LOVE, FAITH,
AND THE
DENTED
BULLET

CAROLYN KLEINMAN

MILFORD
HOUSE

an imprint of Sunbury Press, Inc.
Mechanicsburg, PA USA

MILFORD HOUSE

an imprint of Sunbury Press, Inc.
Mechanicsburg, PA USA

For information about special discounts for bulk purchases, please contact Sunbury Press Orders Dept. at (855) 338-8359 or orders@sunburypress.com.

To request one of our authors for speaking engagements or book signings, please contact Sunbury Press Publicity Dept. at publicity@sunburypress.com.

FIRST MILFORD HOUSE PRESS EDITION: February 2021

Set in Adobe Garamond | Interior design by Crystal Devine | Cover by Terry Kennedy | Edited by Lawrence Knorr.

Publisher's Cataloging-in-Publication Data
Names: Kleinman, Carolyn, author.
Title: Love, faith, and the dented bullet / Carolyn Kleinman.
Description: First trade paperback edition. | Mechanicsburg, PA : Milford House Press, 2021.
Summary: Through letters and diary entries, we learn how a Polish Jew, survives World War II and in 1947 falls in love in with a Mennonite farm girl.
Identifiers: ISBN : 978-1-620064-67-2 (softcover).
Subjects: FICTION / Historical / World War II | FICTION / Jewish | FICTION / Romance / Multicultural and Interracial.

Product of the United States of America
0 1 1 2 3 5 8 13 21 34 55

Continue the Enlightenment!

This book is dedicated to
my mother, Sylvia Gershcow,
for sharing her love of reading with me
and
my husband, Steven Kleinman,
for all his love and support

Carolyn Kleinman

CHAPTER 1

"I SURVIVED. I don't know why when so many others died. There's nothing more to say." That was all Ellen Singer's father, a Holocaust survivor, would tell her about his life during World War II. Ellen was ten years old when she asked her father about the war, and, true to his word, after essentially telling her nothing at all, her father never spoke about the war again. Ellen was surprised she was thinking about this now. She would have preferred to recall a more comforting memory. Yet this is what Ellen Singer remembered right after she buried her ninety-eight-year-old dad.

Ellen sighed. For days, a grainy World War II newsreel had been playing in her brain, so she had to be vigilant. She could push aside the black and white pictures when she was busy. She did, after all, have a lot do. She had a family to care for and an estate to settle. The problem was that the images were stubborn. They were quick to sense when Ellen's mind wandered, and then they deviously attacked. Ellen wanted to relax. She had been so tense at the graveside service; she was physically and emotionally drained. So very tired. The visions jumped at the opportunity and ambushed her again. She wasn't strong enough to resist them. They dragged her to a time and place she did not want to go.

Ellen's vivid imagination was in control. Reality was temporarily pushed aside. She was pulled into a World War II mini-drama, and this time she added sound effects. Suddenly, she no longer was herself, a mature grandmother. She was transformed into a little girl wearing a torn sweater who was cradled in her father's arms. When a guard in a German uniform abruptly wrenched her from her father's grasp, she jerked and kicked to free herself from the fat fingers holding her around her waist. The guard flung her face down into the mud. Ferocious dogs barked. A train whistle blew, and a loudspeaker screeched words made unintelligible by static. Crying. A lot of ragged looking people were crying. Shrieks and crying. Ellen shook her head to free herself from the cascading images. She touched her face. It was wet with tears.

Later that evening, Ellen's home was filled with people who had gathered for a religious service to enable her to say *Kaddish*, the prayer recited following the death of a close relative. She hoped the ritual would calm and comfort her and give her some respite from the terrible visions lurking in her head. She knew her father, Jacob Friedman, would not be pleased that she was observing the traditional mourning rites. He had rejected God and Judaism after the war, long before she was born, but she didn't have to worry about pleasing him now.

Ellen's voice quavered only once when she recited the *Kaddish* prayer in her crowded living room. After the service, Ellen was surrounded by relatives and friends who murmured words of condolence and lavishly praised her father. She heard the words "warm," "loving," and "generous" repeated again and again, and she forced herself to dutifully nod in agreement. The evening ended with a multitude of handshakes and hugs. After the last guest left, Ellen wearily collapsed into her favorite overstuffed recliner. She looked at the matching chair beside her and wished her father, who loved so many people, were sitting there now. She wished she could finally confront him and ask the one question she had been afraid to ask, "Dad, why didn't you love me?"

CHAPTER 2

"ELLEN, WHAT'S WRONG?" Mark, Ellen's husband, was concerned. He had awoken and was surprised to find that his wife was not beside him in bed. Instead, she was curled up in a chair in the family room in the middle of the night.

"Oh, Mark, I'm sorry. Did I wake you?" Ellen asked.

"No. I just came downstairs for a glass of water. What's going on? You were so tired when we went to bed. You should be sound asleep."

"I tried to sleep, but when I close my eyes, I see these frightening images. They began to haunt me after I read the first letter."

"What letter?" Mark asked.

"There was so much to do. We spent so many hours at the hospice center, and we had to pack up and empty Dad's apartment. After Dad died, we had to make funeral arrangements, too."

"Wait. What letter?" Mark asked again.

"Actually, I found a lot of letters. There was a pile of them held together by a frayed ribbon. They were in one of the boxes we brought home from my dad's place."

"And you read them?"

"Not all. Just the first one. The envelopes were sealed and numbered. I didn't have time to read more, and I'm not sure I want to."

"Who wrote the letters?"

"My dad. I recognized his peculiar handwriting immediately. Mark, what really threw me was that the letter I read was a love letter written to a woman named Anna. The same name and address were on all the envelopes."

"Oh, no. I knew the man. I can't believe he cheated on your mother."

Ellen hesitated and then said, "I'd like to think Dad was faithful to Mom, but I really don't know. Maybe whatever there was between my dad and this woman was over long before he married Mom."

"Well, I'm no Dr. Freud, but if the letter you read has upset you so much, I think we'd better look at it together, and we should do it right now."

"But Mark, it's so late. Maybe we should wait and look at it in the morning."

"No time to waste. Come on, my girl, go get that letter, and I'll make us some of that chamomile tea you like. We're going to resolve this tonight, and then we'll both get some sleep."

Mark placed two steaming mugs on the table just as Ellen entered the softly lit kitchen. Ellen was nervous but also relieved. She knew she could count on Mark. After forty-two years of marriage, two children and three grandchildren, Mark was still her hero, the shy engineer who persistently proposed to her until she said "yes."

"Here it is," Ellen said. Her hand trembled as she placed a letter on the table, and then she sank into one of the kitchen chairs.

"Good, now we can get to the bottom of things. Don't worry, honey, it's only a letter," Mark said as he sat down on the chair across from Ellen's.

"But I know what's in it, and that's what has me worried," Ellen said.

Mark reassuringly squeezed Ellen's hand. Then he picked up the letter and read it aloud.

<hr>

LETTER 1

Dear Anna,

I'm writing this letter because you asked me to. I don't write letters. I don't have loved ones to write to. Everyone in my family is dead. Killed by the Nazis. They are all gone, but I still see them. They are alive in my dreams. Every night I promise them that I will not forget them. But I cannot send them letters. Why should I write letters now? You say you think I keep too much bottled up and that writing about my life will uncork the bottle. But you don't understand. The genie inside is angry and resentful. You are very good to me, Anna, but my memories may be more than even you can handle.

I know I've become hard. I had to in order to survive. For a long time, I've not allowed myself to feel or care or soften. I'm afraid of being vulnerable. I simply can't cope with any more hurt, any more losses.

I never thought I would meet someone like you. Someone who would find a way to slide under my tough skin and touch my heart. I never dreamed I would love again. Oh, Anna, I wish you could be "my" Anna, but you tell me that we will only be friends. I don't know what to do. Should I run away from you so you will not hurt me? Or will you hold onto my hand if I grab it? Will you run away with me? I love you, sweet Anna. Why can't love conquer all? Why isn't it enough? It should be enough!

Love me, Anna, as I love you. I will share everything with you. I will tell you the secrets I guard. You know I am Polish and I was in Europe during the war. That much I was able to say. But what I have not told you is that I was trapped in the Warsaw ghetto and then shipped off to the death camp Treblinka. Why did I live when so many others died? I ask myself this question every day.

Anna, I don't feel better right now. I hurt and I feel shaky. I don't think writing helps. I will seal this letter in an envelope. Maybe I will send it to you. Maybe not. You ask a lot of me, Anna. You want to know me, but will you love me if you know everything about me?

Love,

Jacob

⋅⟨◉⟩⋅

"I don't understand," Ellen said. "Why was I so afraid of reading this letter again? The images I see are not described here."

"What do you see?" Mark asked.

"I'm at a train station outside a concentration camp. I'm a little girl, and a soldier yanks me out of my father's arms."

"Well, your dad did write he was in the Warsaw ghetto and in a death camp. Think about it. You've seen countless pictures of those horrific places in movies and books. You probably are recalling those images and placing yourself and your dad in the midst of them."

"Okay. That explanation makes sense. You may be right."

"You know, your dad was quite adept at changing the subject whenever I asked him about his family or his life in Poland. Did he ever tell you what happened to him during the war?"

"No," Ellen said quietly.

"No wonder you were shocked when you read that he had been in the Warsaw ghetto and Treblinka."

"But why did it have to be such a jolt? Why didn't my dad tell me these things himself when he was alive?"

Mark put the letter on the table and leaned back in his chair. "I don't know. Maybe he didn't want to upset you. Maybe there never was a right time. Maybe it was just too painful for him to dredge up the past."

"But don't you see what this means? I grew up thinking my dad was one of the lucky ones, that he was somewhere safe during the war. He didn't have a number tattooed on his body. Now I find out he actually

6

was in a place as bad if not worse than Auschwitz. Once again, I was wrong about my father."

"Oh, Ellen, there was no way you could know what your dad chose not to share. Jews in the death camps were not tattooed because there was no reason to keep track of them; they were immediately put to death. It's a miracle your father survived."

"But how? How did he survive Treblinka?"

Mark yawned. "I don't know. Maybe the answer is in one of the other letters in the packet. But, honey, it's very late. Enough for tonight. We need to get some sleep."

Ellen nodded. "Okay. I'll try. I just wish I had been less obedient and asked my father more questions about his life. I wish I knew more."

Mark picked up their mugs and walked to the sink. "You know," he said as he rinsed the mugs and placed them in the drying rack, "it's a shame that letter wasn't dated. I must admit I'd like to know when your dad knew and loved this Anna. I wonder what she was like. Are you curious, too?"

Mark didn't get a response. He was alone. Ellen had left the room and had not heard his question.

CHAPTER 3

E ARLY THE NEXT morning, Mark was softly singing an off-key rendi-
tion of "A Hard Day's Night." Beatles' songs were among his favorites
to jumpstart his day. Unlike her husband, Ellen never eagerly sprang out
of bed and sang a tune or even hummed one. Mark was wearing faded
gray sweatpants and a well-worn t-shirt. He was hurriedly jamming his
feet into his sneakers when he said, "I'm off for my morning jog. Want
to join me?"

Ellen laughed. "When have I ever, in all our years together, wanted to
run? But thank you, dear, for asking. Go. Enjoy your run. I'll make you
a nice breakfast when you get back."

Mark gave her a "thumbs up" and then quickly pounded down the
stairs. The front door closed with a crisp, loud thwack that signaled that
he was off and running. Afterwards, it was quiet in the house. It was the
time of day Ellen liked best. She had the house all to herself for a while.
It was her "Ellen time." Their suburban colonial was too big for the two
of them now, but Ellen was reluctant to downsize. She liked having space
for all the antiques she had collected over the years, and there was room
for the whole family to stay together when they came to visit.

With some reluctance, Ellen wriggled out of her warm bed. She
groaned, just a little, as she arched her back, slid her feet into slippers,

and then shuffled into the bathroom. This was the part of the morning she liked the least, the first look in the bathroom mirror. She grew up looking like a female clone of her father, the same thin build, long angular face, and dark curly hair, but over the years, she had slowly but steadily accumulated extra pounds. Now that she was sixty-six years old, she more closely resembled her very round mother. Mark told her that he was happy she was no longer bony, that he loved hugging her soft curves, but she found this metamorphosis unnerving. Her raven curls were now more salt than pepper and getting grayer every day, morphing into her mother's pale locks, and her fine chiseled features, so like her dad's, were now a thing of the past, replaced by her mother's full cheeks and double chin.

"Soon, you will take over my whole body, Mom," Ellen said to her reflection. "Dad is gone now, and age is erasing the last signs of him from my face, too." Ellen moved closer to the mirror for a better look and blinked. She still had the green eyes she had inherited from her father, the same eye color she had passed on to her children and grandchildren.

No matter where she started, Ellen's thoughts wound back to her father. There was no use fighting it. She would mourn him differently than she had her mother, but she would mourn him. So, it really was not surprising that Ellen paused on the landing and did not immediately go downstairs to turn on the coffee pot and make breakfast. Instead, she turned and went into the guest room at the end of the hall. She retrieved her father's pile of letters from one of the boxes she had stacked in the closet. Her father was dead and buried. He couldn't answer her questions, but maybe the letters could. She was ready to read another letter.

CHAPTER 4

Dearest Anna,

I wanted to tell you that I love you today, but you stopped me. You said you were not ready to discuss such things. You said you want to know me better first. You asked about my family and my past. I tried to get the words out, but they stuck in my throat. I trust you, Anna, but I feel like I am breaking a sacred bond with the dead. It's hard to share my memories with someone else. I have so little left that belongs just to me.

Instead, we discussed Edgar Allan Poe's poem "Annabel Lee." Its gentle melodic beauty reminds me of you and the everlasting love I have for you. It's also a dark poem and deep. You said that description reminded you of me. I don't know if that is true, but I feel I am in a safe place when we talk about literature, even when we disagree.

You asked if I had started to write letters to release my feelings. I said I had written one but admitted that it was difficult. You pleaded with me to continue, to pretend I was

10

talking to you. So, here I am, trying to continue. I will write down what is safe to tell you about my life.

I was born in 1920, and I grew up in Kaluszyn, about thirty-five miles east of Warsaw. My father was a *shohet*. Anna, do you know what a *shohet* is? In case I haven't told you, I will tell you now. A *shohet* is a kosher butcher. My father slaughtered animals in a humane way and prepared meat correctly for our Jewish community. My father was a pious man. He divided his time between his work and the synagogue. It was taken for granted that I would become a *shohet*, too, as I was my father's only son. I also had to excel at my lessons at the *cheder* or religious school. So, I learned to read from the Torah, and I learned my father's trade. Yes, Anna, that is why I'm still a kosher butcher today.

My father chose a bride for me when I was nineteen. She was from Warsaw. Her father and mine had been friends when they were boys. I was so nervous at our wedding. I wasn't sure what to do. Fortunately, I was blessed. Esther was a black-haired beauty. Anna, you do not look anything like her, but like Esther, you have a generous and gentle soul! Esther was only seventeen years old when we wed, but she was already a great cook and an accomplished pianist.

Esther learned to play on her family's shiny black grand piano. I never had enough money to buy her a piano. I was saving up for one, putting aside a little each week. One of our neighbors had an old piano for sale. When I had enough money, I was going to buy it, move it into our home, and surprise her. I knew she would cry with joy and play and play and that even the gloomiest of winter nights would be warm and lively. I was still saving for that used piano when my world fell apart. The Germans took everything. Oh, Anna, I can't listen to piano music anymore. The Germans took that away from me, too.

In September of 1939, the Germans invaded my life. There was a battle in Kaluszyn, and there were German bombs. Half of my town was leveled. Suddenly, there were German soldiers everywhere, and it was not safe to be a Jew. All Jews were required to wear a Star of David. Anna, I must remember to ask you if you heard about this. In addition, the German soldiers seized young Jewish men and put them in labor gangs. Esther and I lived at the edge of the Jewish quarter. My father begged us to stay inside as much as possible to avoid running into the soldiers.

My mother was terribly ill; the doctor said she had pneumonia. My father, who was considerably older than my mother, seemed to age overnight. He became frail and his hands shook. He no longer had the strength to be a *shohet* and relied on me. My mother coughed all through the winter and died in the spring.

My sister, who lived in Warsaw with her husband and children, came home when we buried my mother. She wanted Father to move to Warsaw and stay with her, but he refused. He insisted that he had to live within walking distance of my mother's grave. A short time later, my brokenhearted father collapsed and took to his bed. He died in July of 1940.

My sister Leah didn't return to Kaluszyn for my father's funeral. I was very worried. I knew something dire must have happened to her or someone in her family. Finally, in August, we received a letter from her. It was delivered by my cousin Saul. Saul had a small grocery store in Warsaw and was traveling through the countryside looking for food to replace his depleted stock. When he handed me my sister's letter, he had tears in his eyes. He said, "Jacob, Leah is exhausted. She needs you." My sister's letter was a cry for help. Her husband Avrom was sick. Leah thought he had tuberculosis. She could not nurse him, care for her four children, and run the family bookstore. She begged me to come to Warsaw to help her. Of course, I had to go. Anna, what else could I do?

I packed up a few belongings. I didn't think I would be gone long. I thought I would return when Avrom was healthy enough to take care of his family. But with the war swirling around us, I couldn't leave my wife and . . .

Ellen gasped. She was finding it hard to breathe. The letter slipped out of her fingers, and the pages fluttered to the floor. She did not bend down to pick them up. Instead, she concentrated on taking deep breaths. She felt very cold. She yearned for something warm to drink but could not summon the will to move. The names she had just read were gnawing at her brain. Those names just changed her world, but if she kept very still and didn't react, then everything would stay the same a little longer.

CHAPTER 5

ELLEN HEARD THE front door open. Mark was home. She knew she would feel better if she talked to Mark. Ellen rushed to the front entryway.

"Mark, you won't believe this," Ellen called. "I was reading my father's second letter and . . ."

Ellen didn't finish what she was about to say because Mark was not alone. He was talking to an attractive young woman who was wearing a modest pale blue long sleeve dress. Ellen noticed that the young woman was flustered. She clutched a bag tightly in one hand, and with the other, she nervously played with the ends of the long blond braid that fell over her right shoulder. It must have been obvious to the young woman that neither Mark nor Ellen was prepared for company. Ellen was still in her flannel checked robe and fluffy neon aqua slippers, the ones her grandchildren called her Cookie Monster shoes because they reminded them of their favorite Sesame Street character, and Mark was wet with sweat from his run.

Mark said, "I was headed full steam towards the door, and I almost knocked this young lady over who was about to ring our doorbell. Ellen, I just found out her name is Elizabeth Landis." Then, he added, "And Elizabeth, this is my wife Ellen Singer."

14

"Oh," Ellen said, "I must look a fright." She ran a hand through her curls to finger comb them into place. "I'm sorry I'm not dressed. I was distracted and lost track of the time."

Elizabeth said, "I'm the one who should apologize. I really should have let you know that I would be dropping by. I have something to tell you if you are the right Ellen Singer. Are you related to Jacob Friedman? He lived here, in Lancaster County, Pennsylvania. Are you his daughter?"

"Yes, I'm Jacob Friedman's daughter. Why do you ask?"

"Oh, I'm so glad I found you," Elizabeth replied. "I was so worried I wouldn't. I'd like to explain if you have the time."

"Of course," Ellen said and waved a hand in the direction of the living room. "Let's sit down, and then you can tell us what this is all about."

Ellen and Mark settled on the couch, and their guest chose the adjacent straight-backed chair near the window. Perched on the edge of the chair, Elizabeth reminded Ellen of a little bird, poised for flight at the first hint of danger.

"This is a lovely room. I especially like all your watercolors of Lancaster farm scenes. They're beautiful," Elizabeth said. "This is a wonderful place. I'm going to be married here in the spring."

"Well," Mark said, "That's wonderful news. Is that what you wanted to tell Ellen?"

Elizabeth turned to Ellen and said, "No. I have something else to say. Now, this may sound strange, but my grandmother knew your father a long time ago. My grandmother's name was Anna. Her maiden name was Miller. Does the name Anna Miller mean anything to you?"

Ellen was shocked and baffled. She knew that name. It was on the envelope of the letter she had just read. That name was on all the envelopes her father had saved.

"You look surprised," Elizabeth said. "You may have never heard of my grandmother. You see, my mother should have contacted your father years ago. She didn't comply with my grandmother's dying wish."

Elizabeth took a package out of the bag she had placed beside her and cradled it in her lap. "These are pages from my grandmother's diary.

Actually, there were many diaries. Gran said writing about what she did and thought helped her make sense of her life. I loved my grandmother very much, and we were very close. I never understood why she and my mom squabbled all the time, but I must admit that my mother is difficult. I love her, I really do, but she is a jealous woman. My mother's convinced that my grandmother loved her twin sister more than she did my mom. I never saw any evidence of this, but Mom believes it. So, when my grandmother was near death and asked my mother to perform a special task for her, Mom was pleased. She thought my grandmother was honoring her, choosing her in preference to her twin."

At this point, Elizabeth took a deep breath. She had rushed through this part of her explanation, but she had been composed. Now, her face reddened, and she chewed her lower lip. There was a long, awkward pause. Clearly, Elizabeth was uncomfortable about proceeding.

"And?" Ellen asked to nudge Elizabeth forward.

"And are you both Jewish?" Elizabeth asked.

"Why, yes, we are," Ellen replied, surprised by the question. "Does that matter?"

"Well, it makes it harder to say what I have to tell you. My grandmother's wish was that Jacob Friedman be given her diaries after she died. If he were still alive, she wanted him to have them, so he would know she never stopped loving him. I was with my mother when she agreed to honor Gran's request, but Mom decided to read the diaries first. That is when she learned that Jacob was Jewish. This was too much for my mother. We are Mennonites, and my mother has old-fashioned views about dating and marrying outside our faith. To find out that Gran had loved a man who was not a Mennonite, let alone someone who was not Christian, was more than my mother could bear. I'm very sorry to say this. You both seem like really nice people, and as Gran loved him, I'm sure Jacob Friedman must have been a wonderful man."

"Was your grandmother always a Mennonite? She never was a Jew?" Ellen asked.

"Always a Mennonite. Everyone on both sides of my family has always been Mennonite."

"Well, Miller is also a popular Jewish last name. I thought maybe . . ."

Elizabeth said, "I know. Everything might have ended differently if Gran had been Jewish or if your father had been a Mennonite. My mother really should have been more tolerant and given your father these diary pages. I was with my Mom when she promised to fulfill Gran's request. I begged her to hunt for Jacob Friedman's address, pack up the diaries, and mail them to him right after Gran died. But my mother said she had promised she would hand over the diaries in person, and that is what she would do. However, we live in Ohio, and for the past six years my mom has always found reasons to avoid coming here. But after I got engaged to a fellow from Lancaster, I told my mother that if she wasn't going to do what Gran wished, I would the next time I visited my fiancé David's family. She gave in because she thought it unlikely I'd find Jacob Friedman now, unlikely that he was still alive. I asked David to help me look for your father. David did a computer search and found your dad's obituary. You were listed as the surviving daughter, and a little more investigative work led me to your doorstep. I can't believe it. Your dad died just two weeks ago. I'm so sorry your father didn't get to read what my grandmother wrote. She really wanted him to know that she never forgot him."

Elizabeth sat very still, and it was quiet in the room. She gave Ellen time to absorb all she had said.

Then Elizabeth added, "But I do have Gran's diary pages here. My mother took out the parts related to our family. Mom said Gran gave her permission to keep the family memories, what Gran had written about family parties, holiday celebrations, births, deaths, and such. Gran also had some family recipes in her diaries, and Mom kept her favorites. However, this is still a thick package. There must be a lot here. I can't fulfill my grandmother's wish, but I can, at least, do the next best thing and give these diary entries to you."

It was hard to get the word out, but Ellen had to know. "When?" Ellen asked.

"Oh, I can give them to you right now," Elizabeth said.

"No," Ellen said. "Thank you, but that's not what I meant. When did your grandmother know my father?"

"I don't know. The diary entries Mom kept are dated, so it's likely the ones I'm giving you are, too. Maybe they will help you determine exactly when they knew each other."

Mark could see that Ellen appeared to be lost in thought, so he took up the slack.

"Elizabeth, thank you for coming today and telling us all this. Since Ellen's father's death, we've been reminiscing and reconstructing what we know of his life. This gift of your grandmother's diary pages may help us learn more. We both appreciate it very much."

The sound of a car horn beeping twice caused Elizabeth to jump up from her seat.

"I have to go. That's David. We're meeting some of his friends for brunch. It's been hectic. There's so much to do to get ready for the wedding, but I'm glad I was able to find you. I sure would like to know what you discover about Gran when you go through these diary entries and your dad's things. Maybe you'll find some pictures you could share. I wrote my contact information on a card and taped it to the back of this package. I know I'll never get anything out of my mother. She didn't let me read any of these entries before she sealed this package up tight. I do hope you'll share what you learn with me."

Ellen and Mark accompanied Elizabeth to the front door. Elizabeth solemnly handed Ellen the package, and Ellen, impulsively, gave her a quick hug. Before Elizabeth walked out of their lives, Ellen wanted to know how Anna's story ended.

"Elizabeth, was your grandmother happy? Did she have a good life?"

"I think so. She and my grandfather got along well. Gran had a beautiful voice and liked to sing. She was always busy with mission work for the church, and she loved her children, twin girls and two boys. And she had eleven grandchildren. We all loved her, and her friends loved her, too. Yes, I think she had a good life. What about your father?"

"I think he did, too," Ellen replied automatically.

"Well," Elizabeth said, "then everything went according to God's plan." There was another short car horn blast. "Got to run. God bless you both!" and she was out the door.

"Amazing," Mark said after closing the front door. "All of that was amazing. And the timing. Who would ever believe that you would find your dad's letters to Anna and then a short time later meet Anna's grand-daughter? I never would have thought it possible. I never would have found it believable in a movie or a book!"

Ellen looked at Mark and her face crumpled. He thought she was going to cry. It must have all been too much for her, combined with her lack of sleep and grief.

"Honey, what can I do? It's okay if you want to cry," Mark said.

Ellen shook her head and started to giggle. The giggles bubbled into laughter and continued to flow into a stream of hilarity. Tears streamed down Ellen's face, but she kept laughing. When she saw Mark's concerned expression, she said, "I'm alright. It just struck me how bizarre this is. When I tell our children about this morning, I'll have to admit that this incredible encounter occurred while I was dressed in my old flannel robe and Cookie Monster slippers. Our daughter, the fashionista, will have a field day. What a morning!"

Mark smiled. He was relieved Ellen was not having a meltdown. Mark had always walked on an emotional tightrope when it came to Ellen and her father, never sure what to say or do after her father repeatedly disappointed her. Mark's stomach grumbled. He realized he hadn't eaten breakfast after his run; in fact, he was famished.

"Uh, Ellen, sorry to change the subject, but is there anything to eat for breakfast?"

"You need to take a shower. While you do, I'm going to quickly dress, and then I'll whip you up some pancakes. Sound good?"

"Oh, yes! And, Ellen, what was it you wanted to tell me when I came in the house? Was it important?"

"I know you're always hungry after your run. I'll tell you over break-fast," Ellen said.

CHAPTER 6

A SHORT TIME LATER, a freshly showered Mark was seated at the kitchen table spooning warm syrup over a small mountain of pancakes.

"How does he do it?" Ellen thought. "He's sixty-eight years old and still lean and trim, all six foot two of him, despite the fact he eats as much food as a teenager. And he's one of those guys who actually looks better with gray hair and wrinkles."

Mark had never been vain. His idea of getting appropriately dressed was to put on whatever his hand landed on in his closet. Sometimes the pieces matched, but often, they didn't. Today he was lucky. He was wearing a blue and red plaid shirt and dark blue jeans that went well together and complimented his light blue eyes.

Mark had finished his first plateful of pancakes and was enjoying his second helping. "When are you going to tell me what you wanted to say earlier today?" he asked.

"Right now," Ellen said. "Mark, my father had another daughter!"

⁘

Ellen explained that she had been reading her father's second letter and was overwhelmed when she read the words "my daughter Rachel."

Ellen quickly summarized what her father had written about his early life and told Mark how chilled she felt when she learned that her father had been married in Poland to a woman named Esther and that they had a daughter named Rachel.

The name Esther in Hebrew is *Hadassah*, and Rachel was Ellen's middle name. Just as Ellen had connected the dots, Mark did, too. Like most Jewish children, Ellen had been given a Hebrew name at birth, a name to use in religious school, in synagogue, and during religious services. Usually, Jewish parents followed the tradition of naming their children after deceased relatives they wanted to honor. When she was little, Ellen had been curious and had asked about her first and middle Hebrew names, *Hadassah Rachel*; however, her father had not told her very much, only that she had been named after special people in his family. Now both she and Mark understood exactly how special those people were.

"Why didn't my father tell me more? Why did my father always push me away? I saw him with other people. He was warm and open. Why not with me? I always felt like I wasn't good enough. Now I know why. I was the replacement daughter, but I didn't measure up. Right?"

"Stop, Ellen. You're everything to me and the kids and the grandkids. You can't let your father's death revive your insecurities. Ellen, you are loved because you are lovable. Believe it!"

"But he had another daughter. He loved another daughter, and I never knew about her. I never even suspected. I wasn't an only child. I had a sister. Maybe if I had known it would have made a difference."

"And maybe not," Mark said quietly. "I imagine Esther and Rachel died in Poland."

"I think so. I didn't finish the letter. I couldn't get past the names."

"But there is more to learn. Why don't we read the rest of the letter together?" Mark asked.

"I don't think I can handle any more surprises today. Maybe we should wait."

"But what if the letter explains how your father managed to get out of Treblinka? You do want to know the answer to that mystery; don't you?"

"Yes, I do," Ellen conceded. "Okay. You win. I'll get the letter."

Ellen retrieved the second letter from the family room and laid it on the kitchen table. She pointed to the sentence that had been so disturbing, the sentence that mentioned a daughter named Rachel.

"Here's where I left off. We can start here. You can read and I will listen."

Mark swallowed the last mouthful of his breakfast, swiped at his face with a napkin, and then began to read out loud.

CHAPTER 7

But with the war swirling around us, I couldn't leave my wife and my daughter Rachel at home by themselves. So, we all went to Warsaw. The three of us huddled in the back of my cousin Saul's wagon, wedged between sacks of potatoes and onions.

Anna, I didn't know that we were jumping out of the frying pan and into the fire. Oh, if I had only known!

Life in German occupied Kaluszyn had been difficult. Still, it was a rural town. It was possible to find food there. In the Jewish section of Warsaw, the ghetto, it was far worse. When the Germans closed the ghetto in November of 1940, the Jews living in Warsaw were cut-off from the outside world. Hunger reigned in the ghetto. I was a man with a useless skill. What good is a *shohet* when there is no livestock to kill? For a while, I took care of my brother-in-law's bookstore. But who buys books when they have run out of money? Eventually, the Germans closed the stores in the ghetto. The soldiers raided the bookstores and burnt many books. I grieved for the loss of so many beautiful, sacred texts.

Food was the only thing of real value in the ghetto. Everyone wanted food, but everyone's food supply kept shrinking. We were luckier than most. Esther, Rachel, and I stayed with Esther's parents; their home was close to Leah's. They had stockpiled some food before the ghetto closed. They had a lovely home, and they had decorated it lavishly with furnishings we could trade for food. An antique Persian rug was no longer worth a lot of money. No, it was worth four cans of beans, a cabbage, and a handful of potatoes.

The ghetto was a prison. The walls encircling it were over ten feet high, topped with barbed wire, and guarded by soldiers who shot anyone who tried to escape. However, there were dangerous ways to leave the ghetto and return. Leah's son Nathan joined the many children who traveled through sewer tunnels and wiggled through drainage holes along the base of the wall to get out and make trades for food.

Anna, I was wracked with guilt. I kept thinking, "I should have been smarter. I should have found a way to get Esther and Rachel out of Poland." My parents were dead, and I was trapped in Warsaw with my wife and child. I also had to take care of Esther's parents, my sister Leah, and Leah's family. And the war was not ending. We ran out of money and had little left of value to barter with. Anna, I will write down the numbers so you will understand how bad it was: Almost 400,000 Jews, about 30% of Warsaw's population, were forced to live in one small, confined area, 2.4% of the city. In addition, more and more people were squeezed into the ghetto from neighboring towns and cities. These newcomers were dirty and homeless. There were so many people, and still the Germans crammed in more and more. Typhus invaded the ghetto, along with other diseases. People died from hunger and disease. They just dropped and died. Every day three to four hundred people died in the ghetto.

My brother-in-law Avrom never recovered. He died, too. It broke Leah's heart when I told her that we had no money to pay the Germans' burial tax. Can you believe this, Anna? The people who killed us by mistreating us had to be paid to bury us. So, we had to do what everyone else did with their dead. We placed Avrom's naked body in the street at night and kept his clothes to trade for food. Leah covered him with some pages torn from one of his favorite books. I had saved as many books as I could before the Germans raided the bookstore.

Every morning, men collected all the corpses in the street, put them in carts, and eventually deposited all the bodies in mass graves. They took Avrom. Leah and the children said *Kaddish*, the prayer for the dead. Leah said she understood why we couldn't give Avrom a proper burial, but she was never the same after he died.

Oh, Anna, I can't adequately describe how trapped I felt. Life in the ghetto was a nightmare. We prayed for the war to end. We prayed for peace.

Then, there were deportations. In late July of 1942, they began. Esther's parents were wobbly on their feet; they were weak from hunger. Still, they were stubborn and proud. They wanted to volunteer for deportation. They claimed it would help us. They argued that if they left there would be more food for Rachel and Leah's children. They said, "It's just a matter of time. We're all going to be resettled in the East." People who volunteered for deportation were given some bread and marmalade; this was a tempting incentive. But I didn't want Esther's parents to go. I didn't trust the Germans.

I woke up one morning and discovered that Esther's parents were gone. They had awakened early and walked down to the plaza. They had joined the thousands who were shuttled to a death camp that day. Of course, we didn't know their destination then. We only knew they were gone. Every day, five to seven thousand people from the ghetto were loaded into freight cars and disappeared.

When the number of volunteers dwindled, the Germans decided to "blockade" areas; soldiers would sweep through a section of the ghetto, assemble all the Jews they found in that area, and march them down to the train for deportation. Anyone defying them was shot. It broke my heart when I heard that Leah and her children had been rounded up during a "blockade" and had been taken away. Leah had left the house that morning with her younger children to look for her son Nathan. Poor brave Nathan! He was determined to trade Leah's last bit of jewelry, a small cameo brooch, for some food. We never learned what happened to him. He was probably shot by a German guard.

I knew it was only a matter of time before my family would be caught in the vice grip of a "blockade." We always kept our suitcases by the door, packed and ready to go. When the soldiers stormed down our street and ordered everyone to come out of the buildings, I was frightened. I feared being separated from my wife and Rachel. I loved them so much. I prayed they would be safe. As the soldiers pushed us out of our lodgings, out of the ghetto, and into a railroad car, I thought, "This is bad, but Esther, Rachel, and I are together. We will do what we must, wait for the war to end, and then we will return to our home."

The crowded train car lurched from side to side. Esther placed her suitcase between her legs and sat down on it. Rachel climbed onto her lap. Rachel had just turned three on November fifth. I remember Esther cried on Rachel's birthday. Esther wanted to make the day festive for our daughter, but we had nothing. No cake, no candles, no presents. I wrapped my arms around the other bag; it was squished against my chest. There was no room to put it down. The railroad car was packed with people. It was very dark. I heard Rachel whimper. I was so angry. The German soldiers had no right to frighten my innocent child!

We hadn't gone far when the train stopped. Suddenly, the door opened, and the dark car was flooded with light. Voices blared at us through bull horns. We were told to leave the railroad car. We were informed that we were at a transit station called Treblinka. We were instructed to leave our suitcases on the platform.

I helped Esther and Rachel climb down from the train. Without warning, I was pushed from behind by a soldier who shoved me towards a group of men. The soldier was holding a rifle. He motioned for Esther and Rachel to move off to the right and join the other women and children who were huddled there. I didn't have time to say a parting word to my wife nor to my child. I tried to keep my eyes on them. Esther was wearing a red shawl. I remember Rachel was crying, and Esther was patting her back. Rachel was clinging to Esther's long blue skirt.

More men got off the next railroad car and merged with my group. Two tall men stood in front of me and blocked my view of my family. I wedged my way between them. I anxiously scanned the lines of women and children, but I couldn't find Esther. I didn't see Rachel. We were ordered to be silent, but I couldn't bear it. I called their names again and again. There was so much noise. Dogs were barking and soldiers were shouting. Guards growled orders. The women and children turned and were quickly led away. I looked for Esther's red shawl, but it had vanished. Esther and Rachel just disappeared. I never saw them again.

Now you know what I carry in my mind and in my heart. Now you know what has broken me. Can you love a broken man?

Love,
Jacob

CHAPTER 8

"ELLEN, ARE YOU okay? You've had a lot to absorb today. I shouldn't have pushed you to finish reading this letter." Mark was worried. Ellen looked very pale.

Ellen didn't know how to respond. She was not okay. How could she be okay? Her father had never spoken about any of this. She had read Holocaust survivors' accounts of the war, and she had visited Holocaust museums, including the large one in Washington, D.C., but this was different. It was her father's story, and it did more than just hit close to home. It was the personal horror of the father in her home.

After a long pause, Ellen answered, "It's all so heartbreaking and sad. So very sad. And Mark, what also upsets me is what Dad wrote at the beginning of the letter. Look." Ellen picked up the first page of the letter and pointed to the words *I will write down what is safe to tell you about my life.*

"Wow. If that was the safe part, then what was in the part he left out?" Mark asked.

❧

The next morning Mark was in his study. He was immersed in an internet search on his computer and singing "Yellow Submarine," matching the beat of the Beatles' tune to the rhythm of his keyboard strokes.

"Auditioning for a Beatles' revival?" Ellen asked as she rumpled his hair, and then she bent down and kissed his cheek. "I'm surprised I slept so late. Why didn't you wake me?"

"You need to catch up on sleep. And besides, we're old retired folks. No need to rush. How are you feeling this morning?"

"Can't believe, after all that happened yesterday, that I did sleep well. I was exhausted, but I do feel better now. What are you up to?"

"Ah, you know me and how I am when I get curious about something. We learned a lot from your dad's first two letters, but we still don't know how he survived, how he got out of a death camp. So, I thought I'd do a little research and learn more about Treblinka. Want to hear what I discovered?"

Ellen cinched the belt on her robe, unconsciously fortifying herself. "I seem to be getting all kinds of momentous news when I am wearing my old robe and bright aqua slippers. Okay, I'm ready. Bring it on."

Ellen moved a chair closer to Mark's desk and sat down next to him so she could see his notepad. Mark had been busy, the page he was writing on was filled with facts and figures.

"Here's what I found out when I checked several reliable sites. Figures vary because people were not carefully counted in the death camps; they were just killed as quickly and as efficiently as possible. Some researchers believe the Germans murdered 925,000 people in Treblinka in sixteen months. And, think about this, Ellen. In 1943 the prisoners in the camp revolted. Only sixty-seven out of the 750 survived. The rest were either killed as they fled or were later rounded up and murdered. Can you imagine that? Honey, I know all of this has been difficult for you to deal with, especially because you need time to mourn your dad's death, but I think we owe it to ourselves, our children, and our grandchildren to learn more. If your father was one of those who survived after escaping from Treblinka, then his letters should be in a museum or Holocaust archive. His story should be added to history. He died at the age of ninety-eight. He may have been the last survivor."

Ellen sighed. "You want to read more of his letters. Right?"

"Yes, but only if you agree it's something we should do."

"Well, you did play the grandchildren card. I guess we owe it to them to learn more about their great grandfather. But there's a risk. We could learn that Dad was some kind of villain and not a hero."

"I think that's unlikely. However, you're right. War can change people, but we can find out together. The letters belonged to your dad, and now they belong to you. We can stop reading them anytime you want."

"Okay. Let's see where this goes. Let's read the next letter."

CHAPTER 9

Dearest Anna,

I was thinking of you all day. It was hard to concentrate on work. My friend Benjamin reminded me more than once that I was using a sharp knife and that I must focus on my job to correctly follow the kosher rules for slaughtering chickens. I was thinking about how we met and how you literally fell into my arms. Do you remember? Of course, you do. Your face turned so red. I know you hate it when you blush, but I like it. You look so rosy and sweet. I can't describe the color. No, it is not tomato red. It's a lovely shade. More like a pale red grape. Please, if you ever read this letter, do not laugh at me. I spent most of the day trying to find the right comparison, and it still eludes me. I daydream about holding you in my arms. I promise not to crush your small body. I dream of stroking your soft blond curls. I hope I will see my love reflected in your bright blue eyes and that you'll give me permission to kiss you. Ah, these are lovely daydreams. You are such a lovely woman! If expressing these thoughts is wrong, I apologize, but I won't apologize for the depth of my feelings.

Anna, I wrote about the worst day of my life in my last letter. When I lost sight of Esther and Rachel, I wanted to run after them. I was so confused and upset. I wanted to know where they went. I wanted to know when we would be together again. I wanted to take care of my family and keep them safe.

I will tell you the next part now. It is so hard to share this with you, but I will write everything down. I feel so ashamed. I should have done something more than stand on that platform with the other men. I was fooled. We all were. Treblinka was not just a temporary train stop. Treblinka was hell. Here is what happened after all the women and children were gone. After all the old and sick were gone.

The men and the older boys stood alone on the platform. We were the only ones left. We were ordered to take off all our clothes and leave them in neat piles. After we took off all our garments, we looked like a bunch of plucked chickens. I didn't like being naked; I felt vulnerable. I shivered in the cool air and struggled to remain calm.

"Soon," I said to myself. "I will be with my family soon. It was so terribly crowded and dirty in the ghetto. So many got sick and died. This is just a place to disinfect people, their clothes, and their possessions."

I watched as a tall lean SS officer approached our group. He had a riding crop in his hand. I remember thinking it odd. "Why does he have a riding crop?" I asked myself. "I don't see any horses." I learned why very quickly.

A man near me was supporting his teenage son. The father clutched him protectively. The boy was trying to stand upright, but he was weak and very pale. After the boy doubled over with a wracking cough, the officer marched over to the couple. In a flash, he whipped both the boy and his father across their faces with his crop. The force of the blow caused the boy to crumble and fall to the ground.

"This boy is sick. Take him away," the officer shouted. A Ukrainian guard ran over to the boy. The guard poked the boy with his foot, and the boy tried to get up. Not, apparently, quickly enough for the Ukrainian. The guard harshly shoved the barrel of his rifle into the boy's stomach, causing the boy to cry out in pain. This was more than the father could bear. He leapt on the soldier, trying to move the gun away from his son. The guard was a large man. He swatted the father away like a fly and shot him in the face. Then the guard turned to the horrified son and shot him, too. I was stunned. Oh, Anna, I could not believe what I had just seen. Two people had just been callously murdered.

The officer calmly nodded and said, "Now you see what happens to those who do not follow our orders." He paused for a moment and tossed that damn riding crop from his right hand to his left and then back again before he continued. "Listen carefully. This is a transit camp. Some of you will be put to work here before you are sent to work in factories in the East. Right now, we are looking for carpenters. Are any of you carpenters?"

Two men stepped forward and a guard led them away. I asked myself, "What is going to happen to those men? Did they just save themselves or condemn themselves to death?"

Anna, I couldn't believe it. I was surprised because next I heard a sound I knew well, the low moaning moo of a cow. Living in the Warsaw ghetto for so long, I had not eaten meat nor seen a cow in a very long time. Yet, there was a cow. It was an old skinny cow; its hide hung loosely on its bones. But it was still a cow. The cow had a rope around its neck, and across the courtyard, an exasperated soldier was pulling on the rope, trying to hurry the stubborn, slow-moving animal.

I realized the officer was speaking again, something about a kitchen. Yes, he wanted a man who knew how to cook in a kitchen, not just over a campfire. He wanted a cook. I was jostled by several men who stepped forward. "Are they all cooks?" I asked myself.

Then, it came to me, Anna. Cooking meant food. A cook would be around food. I might be able to get some food to Esther and Rachel. I moved forward quickly and said, "Wait! Wait! I'm a cook and a butcher, too. You need me. You have a cow over there. I can slaughter it so that you will have the tastiest cuts and the most meat out of that scrawny animal. And, if there is any milk left in that old cow, I will tend to the animal and milk her until you are ready to kill her. I'm a good cook, too." Now, this last part was a lie, Anna. I had never cooked. Esther cooked, but I enjoyed being with her in the kitchen. I used to help her chop vegetables and clean up. Esther was a good cook, and I had watched her carefully. I figured I could make some simple dishes if not too much was asked of me.

"A cook and a butcher, you say?" the officer asked me. I nodded. "Okay, this one," he said and pointed his riding crop at me. A guard motioned with his rifle for me to follow him. I heard the groans and grumbles of the men left behind. Men I never saw again.

Later, this is what I learned happened on that dreadful day. While I undressed on the platform, Esther and Rachel were led to a drab building where guards ordered them to disrobe and barbers cut off their hair. While I was lying to the SS officer and claiming I was a good cook, my wife and child were being hurried through a narrow passage that the Nazis called *Himmelstrasse* or the Road to Heaven. It did not lead, as promised, to a shower room. No, it led to a gas chamber. The Germans even had the audacity to place a Torah curtain from a synagogue over the entrance. It was inscribed with some words from Psalms, "This is the gate of the Lord; the righteous shall pass through it." As I followed my surly Ukrainian guard and left the railroad platform, I heard an orchestra playing. I found out later that the Germans forced Jewish musicians to play tunes to drown out the victims' screams as they were being gassed. While I was given a scrap of soap for my shower, my naked wife and daughter were also given slivers of soap to reassure them that they were only in a shower line. As I cleansed myself with cold brownish water that dripped from an outdoor faucet, Esther and Rachel were crammed into a gas chamber. When the gas chamber was filled, the guards threw in additional babies and small toddlers. Their tiny bodies hit the ceiling before landing on the heads of the helpless women and children. Afterwards, one of the guards yelled, "Ivan, water!" That was the signal for the gassing to begin. And, as I shivered after I washed up and slid my still wet body into some ill-fitting, raggedy clothes, my wife and my child were part of the group that was gassed that day. I was told that the innocents screamed and pounded on the walls of the chamber when they were gassed. And if, by some miracle, any were still alive when the chamber was opened, they were immediately shot. So, as I was being led by my guard to the kitchen of Sergeant Adolph Schmidt, my family died, and I was given the means to live.

I have written for a long time. It hurts so much to remember these things. I do this only for you. Only because you asked. I cannot read about World War II. I lived through it and that is enough. I want to move forward, but I cannot escape the war's hold on me. I still live through the horrors repeatedly at night in my dreams and sometimes during the daytime as well. When I hear a child call for her mother, I look around and hope I will see Rachel and Esther, but I never do. Enough for now. I am very tired. Forgive me, Anna, if I have shared too much. I wonder just how much someone like you, who is not Jewish, can truly understand.

Love,
Jacob

CHAPTER 10

"WHAT ARE YOU going to do now?"

Ellen didn't have an answer. More than a week had passed since Ellen and Mark had read Jacob Friedman's third letter, and Ellen was haunted by the horrific scenes her father had described and worried and confused. She was asking herself questions she felt she ought to have asked from the start. Did her father want her to find the letters and read them? Or had she betrayed him by reading what he never meant to share? Did he save the letters because he treasured them, or were they insignificant, forgotten relics of his past? And what about her father's love for this woman Anna? Why had Anna's diary entries literally fallen into her hands now? Was it Ellen's fate to move forward and do something with these writings, or was she meant to run away from all of this? She was floundering in a morass of indecision. Ellen had been a highly regarded social worker for almost forty years and had helped others make countless important decisions. So why was she stuck? Even though he was dead, her father was still sapping her confidence and making her doubt herself. She simply had to decide and move on.

Ellen knew her two friends were waiting for her to respond and tell them what she was going to do next. The younger of the two women, Sarah, had asked the question. Sarah was a twenty-five-year-old waitress/

36

poet who liked experimenting with her make-up, her hair style, and her clothes. Today her hair and tight spandex top were both bright pink, and she was wearing a short pink skirt that snugly hugged her slim hips. Sitting next to her was Paula in a business suit that screamed, "I am a highly paid executive!" And the suit spoke the truth. Paula, a forty something recent divorcee and mother of three athletic sons, was always on the move to business meetings and team practices in her black Escalade.

If you had asked Ellen a year ago if she would ever bond with these two women, she would have answered, "Why, that's a ridiculous question!" The three of them were so different and had so little in common. Their lives converged after Ellen posted a notice on her supermarket's community bulletin board: Wanted—People to join a Writers' Group (no experience necessary—we will meet in the library's conference room on Tuesday nights). In addition to Ellen, Sarah and Paula were the only ones who came to the opening meeting of the Tuesday Night Writers' Club, and it did not have an auspicious beginning. Sarah showed up in a green mini dress that matched her green hair. She sulked and looked uncomfortable in the stately suburban library, and Paula did not hide the fact that she was disappointed. Paula snobbishly boasted that she had once written a column called "Sorority Chatter" for her college newspaper. Ellen was depressed. These two women were not the quiet, reserved intellectual types she had hoped to attract. Nonetheless, all three did agree to meet again as they all were seeking a writing outlet. Sarah, a college drop-out, was floundering. She wanted to hone her skills and supplement her income with some freelance writing. Paula needed a new stress releasing activity to help her cope with family and work pressures, and Ellen, who had just retired, wanted a creative project. All begrudgingly agreed to write something, share it over coffee at the next meeting, and then decide if the club had a future.

So, it began. No one else joined them. At the end of their second meeting, the three women were wary but did agree to give the club a chance and meet once a week on a trial basis. One week led to the next, and before they knew it, they had become a group. It soon became clear what path each would follow. Sarah's poems and vignettes about her customers at the cafe where she worked were wickedly funny and concise.

Of the three, Sarah was the most talented writer. Ellen discovered that all the hours she had spent watching mystery shows on TV and reading detective novels were not wasted after all. She had an uncanny knack for dropping clues through a story and then tying them together at the end. In addition, Ellen loved the protagonist she created for her adventures, Selma Singer, "a super sleuth and sexy siren." Selma, who shared Ellen's last name, was an indomitable alter ego. Ellen was enamored with the alliteration in her heroine's description. Unfortunately, her writing group friends did not share her enthusiasm for the all the "s" words nor for the clever way Selma could both wear incredibly tight clothes and pack a secret collapsible derringer in her bra. As for Paula, she found her stress relief in highly sexed romance novels, so she decided to adopt a "no holds barred" approach when she wrote her romance stories. Or, as Ellen liked to quip, it was an "all holds bared" approach. To be charitable, although Paula's plots were flimsy, the writing was steamy.

Who could have guessed it would work out so well? The women in the writing group were mutually supportive, and they enjoyed writing. Over time, they did more than just critique each other's work; despite their many differences, they discovered that they enjoyed each other's company. They had become close friends. Writing stories for the club to review had been a lifeline for Ellen when her father was dying. When her dad had lapsed into a coma at the hospice center, the quiet had been unbearable, and she had found a refuge in her Detective Selma's fictional world. This was a world Ellen could control, one in which logic reigned and goodness was rewarded. Selma followed clues, gave karate chops to bad guys, and solved mysteries. Now, Ellen wanted to write another Selma story. She wanted to give her protagonist another opportunity to be strong, smart, and heroic, but too much was swirling in Ellen's head.

Tonight, when it was her turn, Ellen did not have any work to share. Instead, she told her friends what she had learned about her father after reading the first three letters in the packet she found, and she also told them about Anna Miller and the diary pages.

"I really don't know what to do now. I just picked up the first letter and read it and then continued. I realize now that I didn't think this through. Everyone has secrets that are not meant to be shared. I believe this is true for both the living and the dead," Ellen said. "However, I'm glad Mark talked me into coming tonight. I was feeling overwhelmed, but Mark was right. Seeing you two is always good for me. I'm sorry I haven't been able to focus on my writing."

"Well," said Paula, "who could concentrate on that fictional Selma when you've had so much real drama to think about? How can we help?"

"I think you have already," Ellen said as she wiped tears of gratitude from her eyes with a tissue. "Thank you for listening, and I really appreciate your offer to help."

"Good," said Sarah, "so let's get started. You've got to learn more. There are more of your dad's letters to read, and there are also those diary entries. You owe it to yourself and your family to find out what's in them. Just think, Anna's diary might give you her perspective on the same subjects Jacob wrote about in his letters."

Paula nodded. "Sarah's right. We'll help you. We can try to blend the two. We can see if there are dates and events that are mentioned in both the diary and the letters and then match up the sections that go together. It will be like fitting together the pieces of a jigsaw puzzle to see the full picture. I bet if the three of us attack the project we can get it done in record time."

"But, but . . . ," Ellen sputtered. "I just told you that I have doubts now. I don't have my father's permission to read his letters. And Anna Miller wanted my dad to read her diary, not me."

"But you've made your decision," Sarah said. "I know it and Paula does, too. You wouldn't have told us as much as you did if you didn't want us to talk you into discovering more."

"It's a done deal, and we're in," Paula said.

"I'm not scheduled to work this weekend," Sarah said. "Paula, will this weekend work for you, too?"

Paula nodded in the affirmative. "My boys will be with their father all weekend, so I'm free. We can camp out at Ellen's house. I can't wait to get started."

"Hey, stop," Ellen said. "I haven't agreed to anything yet."

"But you will," Sarah said. "Ellen, there's a mystery here, and we want to help you solve it. How did your Jewish father survive Treblinka and end up falling in love with a Mennonite girl in Lancaster, Pennsylvania? There is no way Ellen Singer can walk away from a good mystery."

CHAPTER 11

T HAT NIGHT ELLEN was in her favorite place in the world, lying in bed in Mark's arms.

"So, how did your writing group go?" Mark asked.

"Oh, it was good to see Paula and Sarah again."

"What's going on in Paula's novel now? Is her anguished hero still trying to control his quivering loins and hard manliness?"

Ellen softly giggled. "I never should have let you read the opening chapter of Paula's book. I know you think such descriptions are silly. Actually, those were mild compared to the ones that come later in her novel. Her hero conquers his fear of love, and then the descriptions get really graphic."

"Maybe I should read more. Sounds like it could be inspiring," Mark said as he hugged Ellen a little tighter.

"Mark, before we pursue the topic of quivering loins, I want to tell you something. Tonight, I told Sarah and Paula about my dad's letters and about Anna Miller and, well, everything. Now they are anxious to work with me on a project."

"What kind of project?"

"Well, they have a crazy idea," Ellen said.

Very quickly, Ellen described Sarah and Paula's plan.

"And Mark, they want to start working on this project right away. This very weekend. That is ridiculous, right?"

Mark was quiet. He was taking his time to formulate his response.

"Mark, what do you think?" Ellen asked.

"I don't think their plan is crazy or ridiculous. I think it's something you should do. I think it's something you need to do. And, Ellen, I have something to tell you, too."

When Mark finished speaking, Ellen was amazed that so much had happened while she was with her writing group. Mark told her that he had been on the phone all evening talking with his many cousins. Each wanted to make sure that he had heard that his Uncle Harry had died. Harry had always been Mark's favorite uncle, the one who had spoiled him when he was little and generously lent him money to cover graduate school. Harry had also been the ninety-three-year-old sweetheart of his senior community. Unfortunately, a drunk driver hit his car when Harry was out with one of his many lady friends. His date had been badly battered, but she survived. Harry died in the ambulance on the way to the hospital. Following Jewish tradition, Harry would be buried quickly, on Thursday, in Los Angeles. Cousins from all over the country were planning on attending the funeral, and Mark hoped to extend his visit through the weekend to spend more time with his family.

"So, Ellen, what do you think? I would love to have you come to California with me, but there is that 'grandparent/special friend lunch' event at the elementary school on Thursday, and we promised the grandsons we'd be there. Are you up to covering for me? You'll have to eat lunch with Lucas and the first graders at 11:30 and then eat another lunch with Max and the third graders just a short time later."

"Oh, Mark, I'm so sorry about Uncle Harry. Of course, you need to go to the funeral. And, yes, I can pack two small lunches and eat a bit with each of our grandsons on Thursday. It will work out. I'll take care of things here, and you can represent our family at the funeral and reconnect with your cousins."

"Thanks, Ellen. I hate to go without you, but now you can spend time with your writing club this weekend. Go ahead. Accept their offer. Let them help you."

"But Mark . . ."

"I know what you're going to say. You're going to tell me again that the right to privacy is important. I get it. I agree. But I think I know what really has you worried. Right now, you don't know if your father loved this Anna Miller while he was married to your mother."

"Alright. Yes. That's part of it."

"No," Mark said. "I think that's really it. And it's making you miserable. Until you find out, it's going to nag at you. It may be that your dad was always steadfast and true. That will be great. And if you learn he strayed, you'll find a way to deal with it and move on. So, solve the mystery, Ellen. That's what you do. That's what you have to do."

"Oh, Mark, Sarah said the same thing tonight. She thinks I'm compulsive when it comes to solving mysteries. But do I have the right . . ."

"Enough. Life is for the living. Remember, you don't know if the letters and diary pages are good gifts or bad. You have to open them and read them to find out."

Ellen wanted to stop warring with her conscience. It was wearing her out. Yes, Mark and Sarah were right. She was curious. She had been itching to read the other letters and the diary pages. But as her dad was involved, she felt she had to be careful. Once Ellen started uncovering her father's secrets, there would be no turning back. Tonight, her husband and her friends had given her permission to do what she really wanted to do. She couldn't resist the temptation any longer.

Ellen sighed and relaxed in Mark's arms. "Okay," she said. "I'll do it. I'll call Sarah and Paula in the morning and let them know that the writing club will start working on this project on Saturday."

Mark was relieved. He gave Ellen a gentle kiss. "Good. Now that we've settled matters, let's get back to discussing quivering loins and hard manliness. Okay?"

"Okay to that, too," Ellen said. She smiled at Mark and then turned out the light on her bedside table.

CHAPTER 12

O N SATURDAY MORNING Paula rang Ellen's doorbell promptly at
nine o'clock. She was holding a small overnight bag in one hand
and a folder filled with colored notepads in the other. Paula had quickly
scooped her hair into a ponytail to capture her corkscrew black curls, and
her cocoa colored skin glowed without make-up. Paula's designer jeans
and unadorned V-necked sweater were classic black and looked very styl-
ish on her tall slim form. Ellen was also simply dressed. She had tumbled
out of bed minutes before Paula arrived and had quickly wiggled into her
comfy blue jeans and her "old faithful" faded purple sweatshirt. Ellen's
minimal efforts, however, looked like minimal efforts. At ten minutes
after nine, Sarah, carrying a bulging backpack, knocked on Ellen's door.
Today Sarah's hair was a halo of bright yellow to match her sequined yellow tunic top and bright yellow leggings. Her eye shadow was yellow and
sparkly, too. Ellen smiled after she opened the front door and welcomed
Sarah. The only thing predictable about Sarah was that she would be
color coordinated, but Ellen could never predict what that color might
be. After the trio was ensconced in the kitchen and fortified with bagels
and coffee, it was time to begin.

Paula said, "The Tuesday Night Writers' Club is now officially
in investigative gear, so we need to be organized. I've given this some

44

thought, and here's what I think we should do. We'll quickly skim the diary entries and letters. Work fast. When you finish one, just grab another. Look for dates, events, and key words and phrases on each page, and then record them on one of the notepad sheets I've brought. Next, carefully attach each notepad sheet to the top of the page you skimmed for easy reference. I'm hopeful the information on the notepad sheets will enable us to quickly match the letters to the corresponding diary entries that cover the same things. Are you both onboard with my plan?"

Ellen and Sarah both said, "Yes."

Sarah said, "Oh, I do hope we'll be able to make some connections."

"Well, there's only one way to find out," Ellen said. "I guess we'd better get started. Everything is on the dining room table. Follow me."

⟡

Ellen's dining room table was covered with stacks of papers. Ellen explained that last night she had cut the cord and released Anna's diary entries from their captivity in the brown paper package. Yes, she knew she was being overly dramatic, but she was nervous and was trying to hide it with some bravado. Ellen had been pleased to discover that all the diary entries were dated, so it had been an easy task to compile stacks of entries by month and year. This was as far as she had gotten before, she had to dash off to a family dinner at her daughter's house. Afterwards, she went to her reform temple's Friday night *Shabbat* service. Once again, she had said the traditional Mourner's *Kaddish* prayer for her father, still seeking an elusive solace as she mechanically mouthed the familiar Hebrew words. Her father's first three letters, the ones Ellen had read, were on the table, too, and next to them were his numbered, unopened letters.

Ellen patted the table and said in a soft voice, "We can work here."

Paula said, "Ellen, remember, we're here to help. We can always stop if we uncover anything that's too difficult for you to handle."

"Yes. I know," Ellen said, "and thank you. Thank you both."

CHAPTER 13

A LITTLE AFTER one o'clock, the women returned to the kitchen and hungrily dove into the chicken salad Ellen served them for lunch. While the three dawdled over tea and cookies, Ellen's mind wandered, and she only half listened to her friends. Sarah complained that adhering to the skimming process had been frustrating, that there were many times when she wanted to slow down and read more. Paula said that she, on the other hand, wanted to fly through the letters that dealt with Jacob's war experiences as fast as she could because they were so chilling. Ellen suddenly realized that her friends had stopped talking. Were they waiting for her to respond to something? Had one of them asked her a question?

"Ellen, are you alright?" Sarah asked.

How to explain. Ellen hadn't found the dates she was looking for. She needed to know those dates.

"I'm fine," Ellen said automatically, but after a pause added, "No, I'm not. I need to know when my father met this Anna and if he loved her while he was married to my mom. It's scary because I've always thought my parents had a good marriage. I never doubted it before, but maybe I didn't see what I didn't want to see. So, I've got to get this settled. Did either of you come across the date when my father met Anna? And what exactly happened between them? And when did it end?"

Paula said, "I can help with the meeting date. Sarah and I read your father's first three letters this morning, just to get up to speed, and I know he mentions that Anna fell into his arms in Letter 3. Well, Anna describes their meeting in more detail in one of the diary entries I worked on."

Paula quickly slid out of her seat and went into the dining room. A short time later, she called out, "Found the entry!" and then she returned to her place at the kitchen table. In her hands were several sheets of yellowed paper. "I'll read what she wrote," Paula said.

CHAPTER 14

Market Day in the city. I do love going to the Central Market in Lancaster and selling our produce and baked goods. Rebecca was there today. She is, as Mother complains, a terrible gossip, but she is a good mimic and very funny. I feel comfortable with Rebecca. There are so few of our group left who are still single. I do miss her when she is not working in the stand beside ours. Time passes more quickly when Rebecca is nearby. I like the excitement of the market, and, although I know it is sinful to be filled with pride, I am happy when people prefer our vegetables and goods to those at the other stands. And making money for the family is wonderful, too. The best part of the day is the "down time," when business is slow, and Father allows me time to visit the stores near the market. I love to wander in the department stores. Today Mother had a shopping list for me. I had to match a swatch of fabric she gave me and buy two more yards, pick up one spool of black thread and two of white, and purchase four pairs of socks for Father. I got the shopping out of the way, and then I headed to the library. My sanctuary! The Duke Street library is a magical place. I would be happy to be a bookworm. I would burrow into my favorite books and devour them, and I would never leave the library! What a silly thought! My brain must be as tired as my body from the long day, but I do have more to record.

This morning two middle-aged women stopped to chitchat in front of our stand. One showed the other a book she had just bought at the bookstore down the street. I looked at the title. It was called Letters from the Front—Conscience, Battles, and Liberating a Concentration Camp. *A local woman had saved her brother's letters from the war, and a Mennonite press had published them. I recognized the familiar logo of the printing house on the cover. The women lowered their voices, and I couldn't make out all their words, but I did notice that the taller of the two was crying and dabbing at her eyes with a lace handkerchief. I was stunned and curious. I decided to hunt for the book in the library. I checked the card catalog, found the number for the book, and went to the stacks on the lower floor. Wouldn't you know it? The book was on a top shelf—way out of my reach. Luckily for me, there was a step unit nearby, but unluckily for me, it was wobbly. While I was standing on it, stretching all five feet two inches of me to reach the book, I began to sway. I felt myself falling. And then I wasn't falling. I was in the arms of a man. Oh my! I was so embarrassed. I think I mumbled something, and I hope it was "thank you," but I really can't remember. I was so flustered. My cheeks were burning. The man very quickly released me, and then I was safely standing on the ground. I didn't know what to say or do.*

Actually, I had noticed the man when I walked in the room. I remember my first thought was, "What exactly is he?" He was wearing "plain" clothes, a white long-sleeved shirt and black pants, but I could tell he wasn't Amish as he had a full dark brown beard and mustache. Of course, my brain said, "The Amish have beards but never a mustache." Then I wondered if he was some type of Mennonite. He was sitting at the table next to the bookcase I was seeking. When I put my bag on the table, the one containing the purchases I made for Mother, he looked up from the book he was reading and nodded at me. That's when I noticed his bright green eyes. He had a long sad face, and I thought, "Maybe he will look handsome when he smiles. Maybe not."

It was nice of him to save me from falling when I stood on the shaky step stool and reached for my book, but then he kept standing there. I could feel the heat in my face and neck. I wanted him to leave so I could stop blushing, but he kept standing in front of me. Then I realized he wasn't looking at me. He was looking at the book in my hands.

"This book is about World War II. Why are you interested in the war?" he asked.

The man spoke English with an accent that reminded me of Pennsylvania Dutch, the type of German that the Amish and Old Order Mennonite speak. I have heard it spoken countless times at the market. Usually, I can accurately place people in Lancaster by the way they dress and talk. But not this fellow.

I remember clumsily explaining why I wanted to read the book. I asked the man if he had read it and could tell me something about it.

"No, I haven't," he answered. "I am surprised someone wrote about a concentration camp. I wonder if he told the truth."

I told the man that I would be glad to let him check out the book and said I could read it at a later time, but he adamantly shook his head from side to side and said, "No. You read it. I cannot. Maybe you could tell me about it sometime? Yes, that might be okay. Sometime after you finish the book."

I automatically said, "Yes, I will tell you about it." I couldn't think of a reason not to. Now the man looked uncomfortable and flustered. He said that his name was Jacob Friedman, that he came to the library on Friday afternoons, and that he would like to learn about the book from an Amish girl.

I was confused. I looked around the room. One elderly man was reading a newspaper in the corner, and, in the reference area, a teenage boy was furiously flipping through the pages of a thick book. Where was the Amish girl? Then I realized he meant me. How funny! He obviously is not from Lancaster! I laughed, and the librarian at the desk shushed me.

I quickly told this Jacob my name and said that I was not Amish, that I was Mennonite, that my family had a stand in the market, and that I had to return to work.

50

Here's another odd thing. When I got up to leave, this Jacob got up, too. He handed me my package and bowed a bit. What an Old-World thing to do. And that is when I noticed it. He was wearing a chain around his neck, so he cannot be a Mennonite as we never wear any jewelry. And another thing. Attached to his chain was a dented bullet. Now what am I to make of that?

Enough for now. I am tired. I need to help Father with the milking bright and early tomorrow, so I need to get some sleep. Maybe if the accident hadn't changed everything, I would be talking to friends about my life and writing less and getting more sleep. Maybe.

CHAPTER 15

E LLEN SIGHED. "SO far, so good. They met three years before my
father met my mother."

"So, Ellen, how do you want to proceed?" Paula asked. "It's your call.
Do you want to continue to follow this thread and use their meeting as
a starting point, or would you rather we rummage through all the papers
we have and look for the answers to your other questions first?"

"And," Sarah added, "there are still a few of the later diary entries and
letters we haven't tackled yet."

Ellen paused before responding. It was as if she were reading a neon
sign flashing in her brain with emotionally charged phrases scrolling
across it. *The late '40s and early '50s. Society's expectations. Cultural differ-*
ences. Love but not marriage. Anna in Ohio. Father in Lancaster. Father's
marriage. Anna's children. Marriage vows. Religion and Sin. Family above
all else. Respect and Trust.

Ellen shook her head to clear it, to erase everything as her children
used to do with their Etch-a-Sketch toys, but one old memory resurfaced
and remained in place. Ellen remembered feeling small and afraid, looking at a forest of long legs, and then, suddenly, her father scooped her
up and she was sitting on his shoulders. She was up so high, and she saw
everything. She had a clear view of a whole parade of marching bands

and floats. Her father gave her legs a reassuring squeeze. "Trust me, Ellen. I won't let you fall," he said. She had relied on him then, and she wanted to rely on him now. *Trust.*

"I think it makes sense to have the story unfold in its natural order," Ellen said. "I don't want to mess up all the papers we just organized. I feel less anxious now that I know when my father met Anna. Let's go on. My father didn't love me the way I wanted him to, but I do want to believe in him. I want to give him another chance."

"Good. And I know what happened next," Sarah said. "Jacob wrote about his second meeting with Anna in his fourth letter. And he also wrote more about Treblinka."

Paula looked at Ellen with concern. "Ready?" she asked.

"Yes," Ellen answered with conviction. "I am."

The women carried their mugs of tea into the dining room and settled around the table. Sarah found Letter 4, took a sip of tea, cleared her throat, and then read aloud.

CHAPTER 16

Dearest Anna,

I started my last letter describing the color of your face when you blush. I have been thinking a lot about that color. I like thinking about you and picturing your lovely face. I love the way your cheeks turn from peach to pink to rose depending on your mood. I wish I were a painter and could capture just one of your many colors.

Do you remember how you blushed when you tried to tell me the reason you wore a cape dress? I was such a fool. I originally thought you were Amish! You must remember that. You tried to clear things up the second time we met in the library. The librarian shushed us so many times that we went outside and sat on a bench behind the building. The sun was shining, and it was warm and pleasant.

I had no idea there was a whole "language of clothes," that the way people dress can say a lot about them. You told me so many things. I now know that Amish ladies pin their clothes and that most Mennonite women also dress modestly but make or buy clothes with buttons and zippers. Like the

Amish, Mennonite women often wear cape dresses that have an extra panel to cover the "top" of their bodies. I smiled because I understood what the panel was designed to conceal, and that is when you blushed.

And then you told me about the netting you wear on your head, the prayer covering, and how it is smaller than Amish bonnets and does not have strings. Now that is all I remember. There was too much to take in. I remember you spoke for some time, but I stopped listening to your words and listened only to your voice. Sitting in the sunshine with you was wonderful. I was calm and content. There was nowhere else I wanted to be. I realized for the first time in a long time that I was happy.

Ah, that was a good day. We've had many good days together. I cherish them all. I must admit that I also feel guilty. What right do I have to enjoy life when my wife and daughter cannot? When I am with you, my family is not front and center. You are. They fade a bit and recede. Remembering them hurts. But I must not forget them.

When I wrote my last letter, I told you about Treblinka. But there is more. Much more. I cannot get away from Treblinka. I fear going to sleep, knowing my dreams will take me back to the horror. Is it possible for me to be a person again instead of a ghost, haunting the world but not connected to it? Anna, I will tell you more about Treblinka. I hope you are right. I hope releasing these memories will loosen Treblinka's hold on me. I will tell you what happened and what was said. I will write down everything I remember.

After I told a German officer I was a cook, a guard ordered me to follow him. The guard took me to a kitchen. And not just any kitchen, the officers' kitchen. And Adolph Schmidt was the officers' cook. I remember the first time I saw him. He was staggering around his kitchen with a bottle of liquor in one hand and a spatula in the other. There were four large frying pans on the stove, and grease was popping and sputtering in them. The man was trying to fry potatoes, but they were burning as he was drunk and not paying attention to them. The guard told Schmidt that I was his new assistant, that I was a butcher and a cook. Schmidt sneered at me and mumbled something unintelligible. He was a large fat man, well over six feet in height. His belly jiggled as he lumbered toward me, and his bald head glistened with sweat. Sweat and alcohol dripped from his oversized drooping mustache. He had tiny pale blue eyes, a large flat nose, and enormous loose lips. Schmidt took one look at me and announced that I was garbage. The guard laughed and nodded in agreement.

"Come here, garbage," Schmidt commanded.

Anna, I was insulted, but I felt I had to comply. I took a step toward him. Schmidt threw his spatula on the table. He grabbed me by the neck with his right hand, while still maintaining his hold on the liquor bottle with his left. His stubby fat fingers dug into my skin. He pulled me towards the stove.

"Garbage should be burned," Schmidt shouted. "I must burn garbage!"

The guard's laugh was a high-pitched squeal. I remember the sound of it echoed in my ears as Schmidt lowered my face closer and closer to one of the frying pans. Hot drops of grease hit my cheeks, my chin, and my nose. I closed my eyes to save them from being scalded.

Suddenly, Schmidt flung me away from the stove. "No, you are less than garbage. There is no need to burn you now. I can wait," he said.

The guard looked disappointed when he left. I think he wanted more to happen, more drama to enliven his day.

I thought, "What have I done? I am doomed. This man is crazy, and he is going to kill me."

You see, Anna, while I was worrying about the burns on my face, my loved ones were taken from their tomb, the gas chamber. Their bodies, along with so many others, were then tossed into a ditch, but not before they were subjected to yet another indignity. All their body cavities were searched for hidden valuables, and if the dead had any gold teeth, they were pulled out. The Germans were very thorough. There also was an incinerator where, after five hours, eight hundred to one thousand bodies were reduced to ashes. However, although the Germans continually cremated bodies around the clock, they could not keep up with the number of people killed, so the dead were dumped into mass graves until they could be burned and turned into dust.

While I cowered in Schmidt's kitchen, I am ashamed to say, I thought only of myself and how much my face hurt. I didn't know what had happened to my family. I learned all these gruesome details much later. At that time, I was focused on the angry, drunken lout who kept raising the bottle of liquor to his mouth and, when he remembered I was in the room, kept lunging at me with a large knife. He laughed uproariously when he nicked my left ear, and it began to bleed. But then he bellowed indignantly when he saw my blood on the floor.

"Clean it up. Clean it up," Schmidt shouted. "I only work in a clean kitchen!" He pointed at a bag of rags in the corner.

I grabbed a rag and began swiping at the blood on the dirty floor, but while I worked, new drops of blood fell from my cut ear. I turned to see if Schmidt had noticed, but the sergeant was too drunk to be aware of anything. He had collapsed into a chair. His arms hung limply at his sides, his legs were splayed out in front of him, and his head was thrown back. Despite the fact he was in a drunken stupor, he possessively maintained his hold on the liquor bottle.

I was surprised when a teenage boy, dressed in clothes resembling mine, entered the kitchen from an inner door and gazed with disgust at the unconscious cook. He was a tall skinny youth with long arms. His large nose was sprinkled with freckles, and his bright brown eyes narrowed when he looked at Schmidt.

"Oh, Schmidt is drunk again. The officers won't like this one bit," he said.

"Who are you?" I asked him.

"I'm Aaron. One of my jobs is to set and clear the table. I also serve the officers their food. Schmidt is a fool. He has been warned that he can't continue to burn the food and serve the meals late." Aaron talked to me as he moved efficiently about the kitchen, gathering plates and silverware.

"I'm Jacob," I told him. "I'm supposed to be the cook's assistant, but I don't know what to do. So far, all the cook has done is burn my face and cut my ear. I haven't been given any instructions."

Aaron turned, looked at the red blisters on my face and my bloody ear, and whispered, "Be very quiet, and I will help you. But if anyone asks, you never saw me. You helped yourself. You must promise me this."

I nodded. "Okay," I said.

Aaron helped me wash my wounds. We found some iodine in a small first aid box near the stove. "Use just a little," Aaron cautioned me. "You don't want Schmidt to notice that any is missing."

I dabbed some on my wounds. When I finished, I rummaged in the rag bag for the cleanest strip of cloth I could find and bound that around my ear to stop the bleeding. We moved stealthily about the kitchen, constantly checking to make sure Schmidt was still asleep and unaware of our actions. Aaron smiled at me when we were through.

"Thank you," I said to him.

"You're welcome. That's the best we can do," he said quietly. "But remember, if anyone asks, you helped yourself, and you never saw me. And one more thing, if you want to continue to live, don't go to the hospital building to get medical attention. Remember, don't do that!"

"Why?"

"Because it's really not a hospital. It's where the Germans shoot old Jews and sick ones. It's a death sentence to go there. Remember that. Now, I must hurry and set the table in the dining room. Twenty-three officers eat here three times a day. I hope for your sake that Schmidt has dinner started. The officers expect to eat at six o'clock sharp. They will be furious if they must wait. If the officers get angry with Schmidt, they may take their anger out on you, too. Be careful, Jacob. This is a dangerous place and dealing with Adolph Schmidt is like walking through a minefield. Anything, I repeat anything, can set him off and make him explode."

Despite the fact it was warm in the kitchen from the heat of the two large ovens, an icy fear gripped me. I peered helplessly about the room. Anna, I was very frightened.

"What to do? What to do?" I wondered. I really didn't want to feed the enemy, nor did I want to help Schmidt, a man who had been needlessly cruel to me. Still, I did want to live and leave this place with my family. So, I figured, it was best not to anger my German captors. I noticed that the dinner menu was on a piece of paper attached to the wall. I looked inside one oven and saw that large sections of pork were slowly roasting. In the other oven, a vegetable dish was baking along with some rolls. Several fruit pies were cooling on the table in the center of the room. Fried potatoes were also on the menu.

The potatoes in the frying pans were greasy and black; they resembled lumps of coal. I looked around the kitchen for more potatoes. I found some at the bottom of a large burlap bag in the pantry but not enough to feed many men. Then, it came to me. I could make potato *latkes*. Anna, do you know about *latkes*? They are potato pancakes. I had helped Esther make them for *Hanukkah*, a Jewish holiday. I found some flour and a few eggs, diced some onions, grated the potatoes, and combined the ingredients. I cleaned the frying pans and heated some fresh cooking oil. I worked as fast as I could, keeping one eye on my *latkes* as they fried and the other on the clock.

A few minutes before six, I heard men talking and moving about in the next room. There was also the sound of chairs scraping against the floor as the officers settled themselves at the table. Aaron and another boy named Ephram came into the kitchen. Ephram was short and compact. He had large brown eyes and a shy gentle smile. The boys helped me place the food on large platters before they carried them through the swinging door to the adjacent dining room. I was busy and anxious to get all the food on the table while it was still hot. I had no time to move quietly. However, despite all the clatter in the kitchen, Schmidt slept on, dead to the world. When the meal ended, I was tired from the long day. I was lightheaded, too. I had not eaten in the morning before we boarded the train, and I had not been given any food all day. Before the dinner, I had been afraid to eat any of the officers' food, fearing it would be missed. Now, as the serving bowls and the men's dishes were returned to the kitchen, I turned my back to Schmidt and stuffed handfuls of leftover food into my mouth. Yes, I am sorry to say, I ate *trayf*, food that was not kosher, for the first time in my life. I knew the pork roast was *trayf*, but I was so hungry I ate some anyway and prayed silently to God to forgive me.

Then, I heard a bewildering sound. It was the sound of men thumping their glasses against the table and calling out with each thump, "Cook! Cook!" I didn't know what

to think; I didn't know what it meant. The noise woke
Schmidt. Startled, he sat up. Asleep, he had looked like a limp
marionette, but now he was suddenly upright as if jerked into
a standing position by an impatient puppeteer. He quickly
hid his liquor bottle behind a sack of flour on the counter.
His eyes darted around the room and then settled on me. The
thumping continued, and the cries of "Cook! Cook!" grew
louder. Schmidt glared at me.

"You will suffer if you messed up this meal," Schmidt said.
He smoothed down his hair and straightened his rumpled
uniform before going into the dining room.

When Schmidt entered the room, the men cheered. I
listened at the door as they raved about his potato dish. Once
the cook realized he had been called before the officers to be
praised and not criticized, he accepted their compliments and
promised to make the dish again. I could see he was genuinely
confused when he returned to the kitchen.

"What exactly did you do?" Schmidt asked me.

I quickly explained that I had made potato pancakes for
the officers to replace the burnt fried potatoes.

"Why?" he snapped.

"Because I was sure you would want something good to
accompany the good meal you prepared. When I realized
that the fried potatoes were too burnt to be served, I made
another potato dish. As you were resting from all your hard
work, I didn't want to disturb you." I tried to look sincere. I
hoped my words would satisfy him.

Anna, I have never been quick with words, but when you
fear for your life, it is surprising what you can come up with.

"Hmmm, you are a sneaky Jew. Lucky for you it all turned
out alright. Now, clean up this kitchen. The boys will come in
to help you. I have a headache. I need to go to bed. But I will
check in the morning. This place had better be in order and
spotless. I only work in a clean kitchen!"

Sergeant Schmidt went to the door of the kitchen and called to a guard in the yard. He said, "Watch the sneaky Jews, and make sure none of the kitchen knives disappear." After giving these orders, the guard came into the kitchen, and Schmidt left.

Aaron, Ephram, and I worked for several more hours. The cook had made quite a mess of the room. Nothing had been cleaned or put away during the day. Food was spattered everywhere, and every surface was greasy and dirty. We scoured the kitchen until it shone. The guard, bored with watching us, sat down at the worktable and greedily devoured a leftover piece of pie. He smacked his lips after each bite. Our backs were to him as we scrubbed the pots and pans at the sink. With the sound of running water muffling my words, I quietly begged the boys to tell me if they knew where I could find Esther and Rachel. They each raised a finger to their lips and silently told me to be quiet.

After we finished cleaning the kitchen, the guard walked the three of us to a barracks some distance from the officers' mess. I could hear men snoring inside. The guard turned and left the three of us outside this building. Ephram stepped forward to open the door. Aaron put his hand upon Ephram's arm.

"Wait," Aaron said. "We need to talk to Jacob before we go in."

I did not want to believe the words that poured out of Aaron's and Ephram's mouths. Only the haunted, agonized look in their eyes told me that what they were saying was true. I started to shake. It was all so horrible. Esther and Rachel were dead. All the people on the train, except for the few who were pulled away to work, were dead. Treblinka was a death camp. A howl escaped my lips. My hands curled into fists. I was consumed with rage. I spotted a guard standing by a nearby fence. I started to run towards him. I have never beaten a man, but now I wanted to murder one. Suddenly, I was hit from behind, tackled by Ephram. I fell to the ground. Ephram firmly held me in place. In vain, I tried to wriggle out of his grasp. I swore in frustration. Aaron dropped to one knee and clamped one of his large hands over my mouth.

"Be quiet, Jacob," Aaron hissed. "We know you are hurt and shocked. We were too when we learned the truth about this place. But you can't behave like this. You can't rush off and attack a guard. The Germans are very cruel. Killing Jews is easy for them. If you do something rash, the Germans will torture and then kill you. I know you don't care about that right now, but they will also torture and kill other prisoners, too. They have done this before, and they will do it again to teach us a lesson. And we must live. Some of us must survive this place. We must tell the world what is happening here. We can't let the Germans get away with this. They have to be held accountable."

I moaned. This was a nightmare. I started to cry. The boys held on to me as tears soaked my face, neck, and collar. My body convulsed with sobs I could not control. Somehow, the boys got me to my feet and guided me into the barracks. They steered me toward a bed made of planks. Although I was emotionally and physically exhausted, I slept little that night. I felt dead inside. I wanted to die. I wanted to be with my family.

Enough. Enough for tonight. I can't write any more.

Love,

Jacob

CHAPTER 17

ELLEN WAS CRYING when Sarah finished reading the letter. Her friends heard quiet gasping sounds. They couldn't see her face; it was covered by her hands. Ellen's body was swaying and trembling. Paula quickly moved to Ellen's side and wrapped her arms around her friend. Seconds later, Sarah was on Ellen's other side, adding another supportive hug. The three remained in this position for several minutes until Ellen's shoulders sagged and her body relaxed.

"Oh, my poor father," Ellen said. "It is all so horrible."

Sarah and Paula could only murmur platitudes. There were no words for such tragedy. Ellen sighed. It was a lot to process.

"But he lived," she said to her friends. "I'm here and my children and grandchildren are here because he lived. The letters I read were about his life after Treblinka. How did he avoid being killed in Treblinka?"

"The next letter, Letter 5, continues the story. That was one I skimmed this morning. But do you really want to go on right now? Ellen, would it be better if we waited a bit?" Paula asked.

"No, I don't want to wait. I know it may sound silly, but I feel like I'm experiencing all this with my father right now, and I want to get my dad out of Treblinka. I never knew my dad could write like this. That last letter was so vivid and so detailed. I never knew this part of my father.

Paula, please, read Letter 5 aloud to us. I know from a letter I worked on that my father escaped the camp during the Treblinka uprising, but I don't know how he managed to stay alive until then."

"Are you sure you're ready to go on?" Paula asked.

"Yes," Ellen answered. "Yes, I am."

CHAPTER 18

Dearest Anna,

I feel like a geyser spewing forth old memories. Did you ever suspect I had so much ugliness buried deep inside me? Do you really want me to go on? I can't ask you. I can't say, "Anna, do you want to hear more about human degradation and death?" I can't say those words to someone I love.

However, I have already told you the worst in these letters. Esther and Rachel were killed shortly after we arrived in Treblinka. Since I've written about the worst, I might as well write about the rest. After I heard my family had been murdered, I ceased to care whether I lived or died. In fact, every day I was surprised I was still alive.

I remember my second day in Treblinka. Two soldiers pounded into the barracks and herded the men outside. Aaron rushed over to my side and swiped the rag off my cut ear.

"Stand up straight and keep your face lowered. You don't want them to see the cut on your ear or your burns," Aaron whispered to me as we left the barracks.

Aaron was trying to save my life. At rollcall each morning and each night, the guards examined the prisoners. If they spotted an ill prisoner or one with a bruise, that prisoner was taken away from the group and shot. So, I did what Aaron said. I lowered my face and stared at the ground. I held my breath as the guards counted the men and looked us over. I heard Aaron gasp when a guard pulled me by the arm and dragged me off to the side. I was added to a small group of sick and battered men. I knew when I saw the look of horror on Aaron's face that I was about to die.

"Okay," I said to myself. "Good. I don't want to live without my family. I don't want to serve these killers. It's just and right. Now, I will be with Esther and Rachel."

I was resigned to my fate. I must admit I did not, like many pious Jews, say a prayer to God. God had deserted me. I tried to picture in my mind all the members of my family instead. My thoughts were interrupted by the loud bellow of a bull. No, it was not a bull. It was the cook, Sergeant Adolph Schmidt.

"Wait!" he cried. He huffed and puffed as he ran over to my group, his fat stomach bouncing up and down with each stride. "I need this one," Schmidt said as he pointed at me. "This one comes with me."

With an indifferent shrug, the guard pushed me towards Schmidt. As I followed Schmidt back to the officers' mess to help him prepare breakfast, I heard the guards dismiss the men lined up in front of the barracks and summarily fire bullets into the group I had just left. I heard screams and the thuds of bodies hitting the ground.

"You hear that?" Schmidt asked me. "Those were the sounds of more Jews dying. I just saved your life. If not for me, you would be dead, too. And, anytime I want, I can kill you myself or ask one of the guards to kill you. And there are many ways to die. Some of them are slow and painful.

Some so horrible you will beg to be shot and put out of your misery. Remember that. Your life depends on how well you serve me.'"

Anna, every day was horrible. Every day was the same. I slept in the barracks and cooked and baked in the kitchen. Yes, I watched Schmidt carefully, and I became a good cook and baker. Occasionally, I butchered animals for the officers' table. Most of the time, Sergeant Schmidt was drunk, and he was a mean drunk. He was always tormenting me by swinging knives and cleavers close to my face. He would laugh uproariously if I flinched or backed away. Often, he would pass out before a meal was prepared. Then, I would struggle on my own to finish it on time. When the officers praised him for something I had cooked, he would smile and nod in the dining room, take full credit for the meal, and return to the kitchen in a rage.

He would shout at me, "They compliment the food that was cooked by a dirty Jew. They say nothing about the things that were cooked by a superior German. I will not let you take over my kitchen!"

He would release his anger by pummeling me with his fists and whipping me with his belt. Sometimes the guards saw the black and blue marks on my face and neck the next day, and I became a marked man, pulled from the group at rollcall and destined to be shot. On those days, I would wait and wonder if Schmidt would once again save me or allow me to die. One morning I tried to stand erect at rollcall, but I tottered in my place; I had been severely beaten the night before. A guard pushed me towards the group of disabled men. After the guards dismissed the healthier prisoners, they began to shoot the bruised and sick. Men screamed and dropped all around me before Schmidt appeared and yanked me back to the kitchen. That morning he had overslept, unable to rouse himself from his drunken dreams. I think I hated him the most that day. I was seconds away from dying. I was ready to die; I yearned for the release. He had no right to interfere!

Anna, I fared better than most of the prisoners in the camp. I was not beaten every day. The sergeant would never admit it, but we both knew he needed my help. He drank more and more to forget that he was stuck in a death camp and had not been promoted. He bought a foul-smelling alcoholic brew that the local peasants made. When he was very drunk or hung over, he usually made a sorry mess of the food he prepared and depended on me to save the meal. He would leave me alone to cook and bake, announcing, before he passed out, that he was supervising my every move. When Schmidt wasn't looking, I nibbled on scraps of the officers' food. At least I had that. Most of the other prisoners were continually whipped and beaten and given little food. The workers doing hard labor were fed the least; they were replaced every three to five days. There was a continual supply of fresh arrivals. Workers with skills fared better and managed to live for a few months before dying from torture, hunger, or disease.

Many of the prisoners committed suicide. They couldn't live with their grief. They also felt guilty because they were alive, and their loved ones were dead. It was not unusual to walk into the sleeping barracks and see dangling bodies; men would hang themselves, using whatever they could get their hands on for a noose. That is how Ephram died. He was a gentle, sensitive boy. He could not bear the cruelty of the camp. That and the loss of his family wore him down. He hung himself with his frayed rope belt.

I don't know why I survived when so many died. There were times when all I wanted to do was die. Death seemed preferable to the insane struggle to live. Then, I would remember Aaron. Aaron made me promise him that I would hold onto life as long as I could. He said there had to be witnesses who would tell the world the truth and demand justice for the dead.

So, I struggled to stay alive for Aaron. One day, Aaron was sent to work on the other side of the camp. Everyone in Treblinka knew that was a death sentence. The camp was divided into two sections. The officers and guards were housed in *Treblinka I*, and the gas chambers and crematorium were in *Treblinka II*. The prisoners who worked in *Treblinka I* slept on that side of the camp, and the five hundred prisoners who handled the dead worked and slept in *Treblinka II*. The workers in *Treblinka II* were continually replaced. Sometimes, prisoners were shifted from camp I to camp II but never back again. After Aaron dropped and broke a platter in the dining room, he was sent to *Treblinka II*. I thought I didn't have any tears left in me, but that night I cried for Aaron. He had come to mean a lot to me in a short time. He was killed a few days later. I heard that when Aaron was moving a heavy load of bodies he staggered and slipped. A guard immediately shot him. Whenever I wanted to lash out at Schmidt or just give up, I would remember my promise to Aaron. I guess you could say Aaron saved my life.

I guess you could also say Schmidt saved my life, but oh, how he enjoyed tormenting me! He never tired of telling me that he was the spider and I was the fly in his web. He would laugh when my stomach would loudly growl while I cooked. Schmidt kept careful track of the supplies to make sure I didn't steal any for myself or for the other prisoners. I did, however, find ways to secretly take bits of leftover food off the officers' plates and the serving platters and put them in my secret pocket. I made the pocket from a rag and secured it to the waistband of my pants. I hid the food I stole there. Although it wasn't much, I felt guilty having more to eat than the others. I wanted to share. The first time I foolishly said I had some food; I was attacked in the barracks. The men nearly tore my clothes to shreds in their haste to find and devour what I had brought. It was horrible. They harshly clawed at my body to get at the food. The men behaved like animals, fighting with each other over every scrap of bread and swearing at me because I had brought so little. I could never smuggle enough scraps in for everyone; they would have to take turns. But I knew it was useless trying to reason with men who were starving. They resembled hungry wolves. I am ashamed to say it, but I was afraid of them. I threw my pocket away. I told the men that a guard searched me and took it. Eventually, they stopped knocking me to the ground and pawing at my body, looking for hidden food. I never again brought food into the barracks. Instead, I became adept at stuffing my mouth with crumbs while I worked in the kitchen, hiding them under my tongue and in my cheeks, and chewing and swallowing when Schmidt wasn't looking. Those stolen morsels, along with the meager rations I was given, enabled me to survive. But, when I close my eyes at night, I still see the gaunt faces of the men. There were just too many to feed, and they were all so hungry.

It was strange, my lasting as long as I did. Few lasted as long. I was in Treblinka for nine months. Of course, Schmidt could have replaced me at any time with another man or woman who could cook. My skills were not unique, but as time went by, my place became more secure. The officers began to request my recipes, and Schmidt, who considered himself a skilled German cook, had no interest in learning anything from me, an inferior Jew. After taking full credit for my work, he could not risk bringing in another cook who might not prepare the officers' favorite dishes as well as I did. So, I lived longer in Treblinka than anyone could have reasonably expected.

The other prisoners were suspicious of me. Some thought I was a spy. Can you believe it, Anna? A spy! They had no other explanation to account for the fact that I had outlived so many others in the camp. I think that is why I knew so little about the big escape plan. Many did not trust me. I had heard rumors about a camp rebellion, but I was never invited to join the planning committee. I really did not understand what was happening until I found myself amid Jews running for their lives.

That is enough for now. I will tell you about the escape plan in my next letter. You know the result. I made it out of the camp and eventually out of Europe to New York City and from New York to Lancaster and to you. That is the best part. I met you.

I will try to exorcise Treblinka from my mind and dream of you. I will think only of you before I fall asleep. Maybe I will think about *Moby Dick*, too. Do you remember when we talked about *Moby Dick*. I will always remember the look on your face that day.

Love,
Jacob

CHAPTER 19

"WHAT AN ODD assortment of things," Paula said. "Things that haven't been explained. The dented bullet Jacob wore on a chain around his neck, the accident that Anna mentioned, and now *Moby Dick*. Do you think they have anything in common? Could they possibly be connected?"

"Well," Ellen said, "I'm glad we've gotten to the rebellion at Treblinka. My father wrote about his escape in Letter 6. I skimmed that one. Maybe I just didn't catch the words 'dented bullet,' and the bullet has something to do with his escape. I never saw my dad wear such a thing. He hated guns, and we never had a gun in our house. And I haven't a clue why Anna wrote about an accident nor why my dad was so interested in *Moby Dick*."

"They might be clues," Sarah said. "Clues we will eventually understand when more is revealed. Oh, I just remembered. I can explain why Jacob brought up *Moby Dick*. Anna wrote about the novel in a diary entry. Give me a minute to find it. I will share Anna's words, and then you will know why Jacob remembered *Moby Dick* so fondly."

CHAPTER 20

Friday, September 19, 1947

I met Jacob at the library today. This was the fifth time we've met.

Why am I keeping track of this? No one will ask me how often we've met. No one knows I'm meeting Jacob. There is no reason to be concerned. If I should run into anyone I know at the library on a Friday afternoon, what would they see? They would just see two people talking. I talk to men and men talk to me all the time at the market. Father could find no fault in this. That is all Jacob and I do. We talk. Yes, we talk and talk. I am amazed two such different people have so much to talk about. After I check out the books I want to read, we leave our customary table in the library and sit on "our" bench in back of the building and talk about religion, books, and politics (which I know very little about but I repeat Father's views and Jacob tells me his).

All this started with that book of a soldier's war letters. I doubt I ever would have met Jacob if it had not been for that book. When I remind Jacob that he asked me to tell him about it, Jacob says, "No, not ready to discuss that yet. Maybe next week," So, I have stopped asking. Jacob told me that he is Polish and that he came to the United States after the war. I do wonder about him and his past. He asks me so many questions about my family, but he says nothing about his. I do wonder. I have learned that he is a kosher butcher, and he works at the new kosher chicken plant (which is not too far from our farm). He only works in the mornings on Fridays and spends every Friday afternoon at the library. The reason he doesn't work on Friday afternoons has something to do with the Jewish Sabbath, which starts at sunset on Friday.

Today Jacob was bound and determined to show me why he loves the novel Moby Dick. *When we last met, I made the mistake of confessing to him that I don't like the book. Although I have started it several times, I have never finished it. Today I found Jacob seated at our customary table in the library. He was surrounded by books and magazines. He had several copies of* Moby Dick *opened to selected passages for me to examine. He struggled to keep his voice at a whisper level as he dramatically summarized the tale. Afterwards, he placed one literary critique after another in front of me. All of them praised this mighty classic. I listened patiently. When he finished, Jacob asked me if he had convinced me that* Moby Dick *was a great book.*

His eyes grew wide when I said, "Nope. Too much fish stuff. It clutters the story and bores me." His mouth dropped open. He was speechless.

I thought to myself, "Now, you've insulted him and established yourself as a literary nitwit. After all, he and the critics love this novel."

So, I backtracked a bit and said, "But, really, it's okay if you like boring fish stuff. Lots of people do." I knew the minute I said those words that they hadn't come out right. My side of the conversation was going from bad to worse. Jacob clapped a hand over his mouth and began to sputter.

"Oh no," I thought, "this fellow is going to explode over a book!"

I was shocked and surprised when Jacob grabbed my hand and pulled me to the stairwell. After he quietly shut the reading room's door to the stairs, he released rolling rounds of laughter. Only then did I realize that he wasn't angry after all. He was just trying to be thoughtful; he didn't want his laughter to disturb the people in the library. He smiled at me and said he appreciated my "candor and insight." Yes, those were the words Jacob used. I am so relieved. He values my opinions.

Jacob told me that he enjoys matching wits with his friends. So, I guess that is what we are. We are friends who can agree and disagree. At least, I think that is what we are. Just friends. But why do I keep thinking about those few short moments when Jacob held my hand? His hand is callused from his work. It felt warm and strong. Why do I keep thinking about the way he firmly clasped my hand?

CHAPTER 21

"YOU KNOW," SAID Ellen, "that sounds familiar. My dad wrote the words "boring fish stuff" in Letter 6. He wrote about a book, but I didn't realize he meant *Moby Dick* until now. I'll read you his take on this *Moby Dick* discussion with Anna. The rest of the letter covers how the prisoners planned and carried out the Treblinka escape."

❧◉❧

LETTER 6

Dearest Anna,

Do you remember when I tried to show you the glories of one of my favorite books? You were so hesitant, afraid of offending me and expressing your opinion. You're a clever woman. You reduced a classic novel to "boring fish stuff." Here I had been trying to sway you with serious well-founded arguments, and you so quickly dismissed them with one sharp cut. I was struggling to remain focused that day, to talk only about literature and not about my feelings for you. You looked so beautiful. You weren't aware of the effect you were having on me. The soft reading lights in the library created a halo around you. After you so charmingly disarmed me with your words, I had to grab your hand and run. So many feelings were bubbling inside me and rising to the surface. I needed a safe place to release my laughter and joy. When I held your hand, I immediately knew that my feelings were real. Your hand felt so right in mine. Your hand belongs in mine. I know you will think me foolish, but I knew for sure that day, that instant, that I love you! My love for Esther grew slowly and quietly. She was chosen for me. You literally fell into my arms, and you are the one I choose.

I have written so much about Treblinka to release my demons. I have done this for you, Anna. Maybe you are right. It has helped a bit, but I still have nightmares about the war. I will write about the rebellion in this letter. I will try to shed more of my memories. First, you need to understand how Treblinka was fortified and why escaping was so difficult.

When I was there, three layers of barbed wire fencing circled Treblinka, and it had six watchtowers manned by armed guards. In addition, there were always guards around, monitoring the prisoners' work and watching the barracks. Nonetheless, small groups of prisoners still tried to escape, digging tunnels or devising ways to cut through the fences. Those who were caught were brought back to camp, tortured in front of the rest of us, and then hung. In addition, to teach us a lesson, ten prisoners were randomly selected and shot for every successful escapee. It was brutal, Anna. It was a hopeless place.

In February of 1943, the mood in the camp changed. Those of us who worked in the officers' mess overheard the Germans discussing their army's defeat at Stalingrad. Word of this spread quickly through the camp. Suddenly, an Allied victory seemed like a real and imminent possibility. We were overjoyed, and we were afraid. What would happen to us?

Around this time, the number of Jews arriving at the camp began to decline; most of the Jews in the area had already been killed. Rumors flew from mouth to mouth. What would happen if the Germans closed Treblinka? Would they kill all the remaining Jews before they left? What was the wisest thing to do, wait to be liberated or stage a rebellion?

After the Germans emptied the Warsaw ghetto in May of 1943, the last of the Jews confined there were shipped to Treblinka. Now there were prisoners in the camp who had taken part in the ghetto uprising. These Jews were not compliant; they were fighters, and they inspired many in the camp to fight back, too. What did we have to lose if we were all going to be murdered soon?

Our desire for action and revenge kept growing. It was as if the camp was vibrating. Thank goodness the Germans didn't sense that something momentous was about to occur. The date of the escape was August 2, 1943.

I wish I could accurately tell you what happened, but I can't. All I clearly remember is hearing explosions. As usual, I was working in the kitchen. Schmidt was not in camp; he had gone to Warsaw to purchase some supplies. After the first explosion, the Ukrainian guard who had been drinking coffee in the kitchen bolted out the door and did not return. I looked out the window to see what was going on. I saw prisoners running in all directions. Women and men were screaming and running randomly about. I heard two words repeated over and over, "camp escape." I saw Jews brandishing guns, knives, shovels, and pitchforks. Dust kicked up by many feet blurred my vision. I thought I must be dreaming.

Anna, I left the kitchen and was swept up into a mass of people, all running fast. There was so much noise and confusion. Guards rapidly fired guns from the watchtowers. Buildings were burning. People screamed names, looking for friends and family members. I just moved with the crowd, and we moved toward a break in the eastern fences. Blankets, clothes, and boards had been thrown over all the barbed wire. The fences had been trampled by so many that we just stepped on the boards and climbed over them. I heard people fall behind me, mowed down by machine gun fire. I kept running. I didn't look back. I was afraid to. I just kept moving. I was very certain that this was my only chance to get out of Treblinka. I followed a large group, maybe a hundred people, across a plain. We moved toward a stand of trees.

After we reached it, we scattered, instinctively fearing we would be a large target if we stayed together. The Germans chased us across the plain; they were in cars and mounted on horses. They never stopped firing their guns at us. I ran beside a man who had a rifle. We were panting for breath. We collapsed behind a fallen tree to rest. He shot at the Germans until he ran out of bullets. Suddenly, he fell forward, most of his head had been shot away.

Anna, I was shocked and frightened. I ran from him. I ran until my sides hurt so much, forcing me to stop. I expelled in retching gasps the small amount in my stomach. I wiped my face with my sleeve, regretting the loss of the little food I had in me. It was then I realized I had a knife in my hand. I had been slicing bread before I left the kitchen, and I still had the knife in my hand. I shook my head, amazed at my own stupidity. Yes, I had the knife, but why hadn't I thought to take the bread, too? I looked around. I was alone. I heard voices and the sound of running footsteps in the distance, but I was alone.

I spotted a tree with low hanging limbs and hoisted myself up to stand on one. When I was confident it would bear my weight, I climbed to the next limb and the next, high enough to see the camp and the plain littered with blood spattered bodies. There were still explosions coming from Treblinka. The sky was gray, and the sun was setting. I had lost all track of time.

Much later I was told that the Jews battled with the
Germans for more than six hours. I don't know if you can
count it a victory when so many died. There were around
750 prisoners in the camp that day. I read somewhere that
about one hundred never tried to leave the camp; I guess
they had given up or were too dazed or weak to try to escape.
They were all murdered a short time later. Most of the two
to three hundred prisoners who made it to the forest were
hunted down and killed. The Polish peasants living in the area
turned many over to the Germans. So many Jews were killed
in Treblinka. Just a small number survived. A few months
after the massive escape, the Germans leveled the camp and
planted trees on the site. Can you imagine it, Anna? They
tried to make it look like an ordinary farm. But nothing can
ever erase Treblinka from my mind. Absolutely nothing.

Tomorrow is Friday. I will work in the morning. My fellow
shohets will go to the train station after work and return to
their families in Philadelphia and New York for *Shabbat*. For
them, Lancaster is just a place to work. I will, as usual, ride
along with them into the city, but I have no family to return
to. I was so alone until you dropped into my life. I live alone
and spend the weekends alone in the cottage I rent. I'd like to
you to see it. Would it be proper to invite you to my house
for dinner? Will you come?

Love,

Jacob

CHAPTER 22

S ARAH SAID, "I hope if Jacob asked Anna to dinner that he knew to include a relative or friend in the invitation. My grandmother told me stories about dating when she was young. Teenage Mennonite boys had cars to drive and were given some freedom to roam. Girls, on the other hand, were always supervised."

"Does Anna remind you of your grandmother?" Paula asked.

"Yes, she does," Sarah said. "Like Anna, my grandmother grew up on a Mennonite farm, but my grandmother wouldn't have been comfortable having a man who was not her fiancé hold her hand. In my grandmother's church, if a boy and girl wanted to hold hands while they were ice skating, both had to be wearing mittens. Today some Mennonite congregations are still strict. If you are caught smoking, drinking, or swearing, you must leave the church. Others are more liberal. In my church, women are allowed to wear pants, and they're not required to wear the prayer covering on their heads."

"You and Ellen are lucky," Paula said. "You both have always lived in Lancaster and understand how things work here. You must remember I grew up in New York City. If it wasn't for the Fresh Air Fund, I probably wouldn't be here today."

"I know about the Fresh Air Fund. That group brings city kids to the country in the summertime. Right?" Sarah asked.

"Yes," Paula said, "and I'll always be grateful to them. I was ten years old the first summer I came here. My host family lived on a farm, and I had never been on a farm. I didn't realize I had put my milking stool next to a bull till I got yanked out of harm's way. The family chuckled over that at dinner and really roared when I said, 'I feel comfortable here. Your next-door neighbors in the dark suits and hats are Hasidic Jews just like mine are in New York.' Now, seriously, who knew about the Amish in my neighborhood? And I'm still learning about them and the Mennonites."

Paula laughed, and Sarah and Ellen joined her.

"Well," Sarah said. "I have to admit that I never had a Jewish friend before I met Ellen. I knew there were some synagogues here in Lancaster, but they were just buildings I passed and didn't mean much to me. I think there were a few Jewish kids in my high school, but I never knew one. Or maybe I did, but we were never close enough to talk about religion. So, my knowledge of Jews was limited to what I learned from reading *The Diary of Anne Frank* in middle school. That's why I understand how Anna felt when she became Jacob's friend. It's confusing when you meet someone who's very different than you are, but it's also fun and interesting. That's why I like sharing my writing with both of you. You both are so 'not me' and see the world so differently."

Paula laughed again. "Oh, Sarah, I think there's a compliment in there. Thank you. I will confess I wasn't sure how the two of you would feel about me because I'm black. Sarah, are you going to tell me I'm your first black friend, too?"

"Well, yes. But don't blame me. I just don't run into many black people where I live and work, and there are so few African Americans living in Lancaster," Sarah said.

Paula said, "Yes, the number is small, just five percent of the county's population. I knew it would be challenging for my boys to be different, but I moved here after my divorce because I wanted to live near my Fresh Air Fund family. They invited me to return to their farm every summer when I was a kid. I didn't love the manure or the chores, but I loved the people. We've remained close, and I often came back to Lancaster to visit them. They were good to me when I was little, and they're good to me now. After my parents died and my marriage fell apart, I wanted some stability and love for me and my boys. I found it right here, and I'm lucky because I also found a good job and then the two of you."

Ellen had been quiet during this exchange. The conversation had taken an unexpected turn and had veered far away from the horrors of Treblinka and the escape her father had described in his letter. Maybe Anna's and Jacob's writings were a gift after all, triggering memories and enabling her friends to share their own stories. Ellen remembered a picture of a tree she had drawn when she was five years old. Her mother had pointed to the branches where there were people peeking out of nests. Ellen explained that the people were her friends, and the nests were their friendships. Her mother had proudly repeated the story over and over. At the time, Ellen couldn't understand why. The drawing was nothing special. Ellen just drew what she felt. It was all remarkably simple. However, now Ellen was much older and realized good friendships could not be taken for granted. There was nothing simple about building and keeping comforting nests.

"Thank you both for being here," Ellen said. "I couldn't ask for better helpers." Ellen wanted to say more, but she knew she needed to remain on task, or she would crumble. She had to get through enough of her father's letters to get him out of the war, out of Europe, and to a safe place before the day ended. Of course, her brain knew this wouldn't alter the past and didn't make any sense, but there was no way she could win a rational argument with her emotions right now.

"Where did we leave off? What's next?" Ellen asked.

"I remember Anna did write something about Jacob asking her to dinner at his home. I'll find that entry and read it aloud and get us back on track," Paula said.

CHAPTER 23

Friday, September 26, 1947

How could I have doubted it? Jacob is very handsome. Most of the time he looks sad, but when he smiles, his eyes shine, and his face softens, and then he radiates so much warmth. It is such a wonderful transformation! I marvel at it every time it occurs. I am so happy when I say or do something that makes him smile. He seldom laughs, but when he does, I feel like I have won a valuable prize. I have never known anyone like Jacob before. I have never known a Jewish person before. Jacob says he is Jewish, that is who he is, and no one can take that away from him. But he no longer believes in his religion. He no longer believes in God. I find this very confusing. I can't imagine turning away from God and all the teachings that have guided me. How can you marvel at the sunrise and be awed by the beauty of a sunset and not believe in God?

Because I only have a couple of hours on Fridays before I must return to the market, Jacob and I do not waste any time when we talk. We rush from one subject to another and never seem to run out of things to say. I have never felt so at ease with anyone. For the first time, I feel someone is really listening to me and valuing what I say. I don't have to just repeat what I have been taught. I don't have to say what I think people want me to say. I can safely express my thoughts, and I can change my mind, too. It is exhilarating!

This Friday with Jacob started like all the others. We met at "our" table in the library, and then we moved outside to "our" bench to talk. I brought along some sugar cookies from our market stand, and Jacob and I nibbled on them. I could tell that Jacob was nervous. He said he had something important to ask me. I thought he finally wanted to discuss the book about the war I read. But no. He surprised me. He invited me to dinner at his home. A dinner for just the two of us!

I didn't know how to respond to his invitation. I was speechless. Jacob misunderstood and assured me that he was a good cook and that it would be a fine meal. I was still silent, and Jacob turned away. He was hurt. I rushed to explain that company always ate with the whole family. I told him even box supper socials were never private. I could see he was confused and didn't know what I was talking about. I explained how this fundraiser works, that boys bid on the meals girls prepare and put into boxes. Afterwards, the highest bidder gets to eat what is inside the box with the girl who packed it. This is, however, never a private meal as all the couples are always in sight of one another. Next, I launched into the story of my first box supper when I was fourteen years old. I confessed that the boy who bought my meal yelped when he saw what was inside my box. In my haste to get to the box supper on time, I grabbed a large shoe box off the kitchen table. Unfortunately, I brought the box containing my father's new work shoes and not the one holding all the food I had carefully prepared. Well, I'm glad that embarrassing mistake was finally good for something because it made Jacob smile.

Jacob was persistent. He said, "All will be proper. I only want you to see my home and share a dinner with me." I said, "No. I'm sorry. I can't" over and over. He said he was disappointed and that he hoped I would change my mind. He said dinner would be ready for me at six tomorrow night just in case I decided to come. I said it was impossible, and he said everything is possible.

Of course, I can't go. I can't.

⊷⧫⊶

"Was that the end of it, or did she go?" Sarah asked.

"I think one of the diary entries I skimmed this morning will answer that question," Ellen said. "Based on the date and this dinner invitation, I think it fits into the story right here. I'll read what Anna wrote on September 27th, the next day."

CHAPTER 24

Saturday, September 27, 1947

It is all Cousin Mary's fault. I have never liked Cousin Mary. Such a meddlesome crow! Mother copes with her because Mary is her first cousin, but I wish Mary would just leave me alone. Cousin Mary dropped by when we were finishing lunch to tell us all about her daughter's engagement and the upcoming wedding. She said she needed Mother's help, but I knew the purpose of the visit was to brag while pretending to be humble. She lavishly praised Mother's wonderful flower arrangements and bemoaned her own ordinary efforts. Only Mother could create floral decorations beautiful enough for her beautiful daughter. Really? I knew what she was thinking as she smiled and preened and laughed too loud—"My lovely daughter Jane, two years younger than your plain Anna, is marrying the most desirable boy around. Of course, there is no way you can top that!"

I couldn't stand it. Poor Father barely had time to finish his last bite of pie before I grabbed his plate and fork and hurriedly cleared the table. I thought I would be safe in the kitchen, but Cousin Mary followed me. She said she was only getting a glass of water, but I knew better when she patted my arm and said, "There, there, Anna. You may not be as pretty as my Jane or your sister Katie, but I'm sure there's a nice Mennonite boy out there for you, too."

I was shocked that she said Katie's name. No one in the family mentions Katie to me. The plate I was rinsing in the sink slipped out of my hands and broke. I ran out of the kitchen and up to my room. Cousin Mary's shrill indignant words followed me, "What? What did I say, Anna? You're twenty years old. It's about time you pulled yourself together and thought of boys and marriage. That's the normal thing to do."

I was furious. Angry with Cousin Mary and angry with myself for letting her get to me. Mother came into my room and tried to smooth things over. She told me I could borrow Father's car. She suggested I visit "that gossipy Rebecca from the market." Mother said, "Go ahead. Have a fun afternoon. Laugh a bit with Rebecca." I wanted to get away, so I agreed, but when I started driving, I didn't head towards Rebecca's farm. I was too upset. Rebecca would see my red eyes and splotchy face and know I had been crying. Rebecca would poke and prod till she found out what was bothering me. I didn't want to see Rebecca. I just drove, turning without thought and looking at the leaves on the trees that were beginning to show off their fall hues.

Suddenly, a streak of color flew in front of me. I slammed on the brake. I heard a terrible crunch. It was a boy. No, two boys on bicycles. They were now standing on the side of the road, and one was leaning on a bicycle. The other was holding a twisted piece of metal. Thank goodness, they were not hurt. I was alright but very frightened. I never saw them coming. I could have killed a boy! Maybe two boys! I curled my fingers tightly around the steering wheel. I was shaking so hard. I heard a voice, and then someone was knocking on the window. I heard, "Are you alright? Are you alright?" I couldn't open my mouth to answer. I felt a rush of air. Someone had opened the driver's side door. Someone was prying my fingers off the steering wheel and murmuring something. Nothing made any sense. Jacob was there. Jacob gently nudged me out of the car. Was I dreaming?

I don't remember how I got to the couch in Jacob's cottage. I felt so cold, so very cold. Jacob draped an afghan around my shoulders and handed me a cup of hot tea. I don't know when he made the tea. My teeth were

*chattering. Jacob guided the cup to my lips, and, finally, I took a sip. I was
so grateful for its warmth.*

*Jacob said, "You've had a bad scare. I've told those Weaver boys not to
race down the driveway. They forget that a car can come by at any time,
even on a quiet road."*

*I remember each of his words because I was concentrating so hard on
them. I was determined to listen very carefully. I had to make sense of all
this. I couldn't believe it. I was in Jacob's cottage.*

"Are the boys okay? Were they hurt?" I asked.

"They're fine. They had a scare, too, but they're fine," Jacob said.

*I asked him over and over if he was sure they were okay, and he said he
was sure.*

*This was unbelievable. I thought I had been randomly driving
around, but I drove down Winding Hill Road. I knew the Weavers' farm
was on Winding Hill Road. I knew that Jacob was renting the Weavers'
grandparents' house. Had I hoped to get a glimpse of Jacob's cottage behind
the main house? Had I hoped to see Jacob? Maybe.*

*I felt very tired. Too much was happening all at once. I needed to go
home and sort things out. I stood up to leave, but Jacob put a hand on my
shoulder. He told me I should wait a bit before getting back in the car. I
still felt shaky, so I sat down. Jacob said he would bring me something sweet
to eat, that it would help me to recover from the shock. He left me alone in
the front room.*

*I looked around me for the first time. There were books everywhere!
Bookcases lined every bit of wall space. Rather than having traditional
coffee or end tables, Jacob had filled wooden crates with books and topped
them with flat pieces of glass to form tables. There were books piled on these
"book tables," too. I was amazed. It was like being in a cluttered library.
But it was cozy. There was a large rug crafted from multicolored rags on the
floor, and an Amish quilt covered the couch. Sunshine streamed through
the windows and gave the oak bookcases a golden glow. On one side of the
room, there was a dining area, and a table had been set for a guest. It was
covered with a linen cloth, and in the center was a vase of flowers bordered*

by two candlesticks. The table had been set for me. Dear sweet Jacob. He never gave up hoping I would come to dinner.

Jacob reappeared with a tray. He put it on one of the "book tables," within easy reach of the couch. Some type of pastry was on a plate.

I told Jacob I loved the room because it was filled with books. Jacob said that his landlords couldn't understand why he needed so many books. They thought he was crazy, but Jacob said, "Books make me feel good. The more books, the better I feel." I understood completely.

"But why," I asked him, "with so many books, do you need to go to the library?"

He told me he went to read the newspapers and to look at the books on the "new books" shelf. And, he added, "Now, I go to see you."

I had never seen a grandparent home like this one. Jacob explained that the bookshelves were his idea, that the cottage didn't have any when he moved in. Jacob told me he was lucky that Isaac Lapp, an Amish farmer and carpenter who lives nearby, had agreed to give him nails, supports, and odd pieces of wood. In exchange, Jacob helped him with farm chores. I had to hide a smile. Just last week, Isaac Lapp had bragged to my father that he had made the deal of the century, that he had found a farmhand willing to do hard labor in exchange for scraps of wood. But as Jacob was happy with the arrangement, I didn't tell him that Lapp was taking advantage of him.

I slowly walked around the room, randomly reading titles and authors' names. I was trying to figure out how the books were organized. Paperbacks and hardcover books shared the same shelves, and some shiny new books were next to some old editions. Mixed in with books that had English titles were books in foreign languages.

I told Jacob that I was overwhelmed and asked him how he kept track of all his books. He said they were arranged by subject. Every room was filled with books of a designated genre. I was enchanted. It was perfect! All those books perfectly shelved, waiting to be read and reread.

"A house of books. I cannot believe it. I could live here forever," I blurted. Oh, did I blush!

Jacob smiled. "That could be arranged," he said. "I have wanted to tell you how I feel about you for some time."

"Oh, no. Not now," I thought. I returned to the couch and reached for one of pastries on the tray and pushed most of it into my mouth. I chewed carefully. I wanted to buy some time. I did not want Jacob to talk about feelings, so I asked Jacob about the delicious cookie. He said it was called rugelach, *a Polish treat.*

I ate another piece of rugelach *and then another and then another.*

Jacob said, "Be careful. You'll spoil your dinner. I've made a wonderful dinner for you."

I suddenly became aware of the smell of food. The cottage was filled with mouthwatering aromas I hadn't paid attention to before, the distinctive fragrance of a slow cooking roast, the comforting smell of fresh baked bread, and the scents of cinnamon and baked apple coming from a pie.

I swallowed my last bite of rugelach *and told Jacob that I was very complimented that he had gone to so much trouble to prepare a dinner for me, but it was impossible. I couldn't stay.*

He kept saying, "But you are here. It's possible."

I explained that it was all accidental. I hadn't meant to come. If it hadn't been for the boys racing their bicycles, I wouldn't be in his home.

"No," Jacob said. "I don't believe that. You came to me. You are here. It's time we talked about us."

I begged Jacob not to say anything more, that there could be no "us." I explained that too many things would always keep us apart. I had responsibilities. My family, my community, and my religion were important to me. We had become friends, and we could be good friends. But never anything more. Never.

Jacob looked so hurt, so very sad. I knew I should leave, but I couldn't abandon Jacob and leave him like that. He had always been kind, and now I was hurting him.

"Then tell me why?" Jacob asked. "Why were you driving down Winding Hill Road?"

So, I told him. I told him about Cousin Mary's visit and my need to bolt when I heard my sister's name. I could see that Jacob didn't understand and was not satisfied. I felt I had no choice. I told him what happened to Katie. It was difficult. I haven't said her name aloud since the funeral.

I explained that my younger sister Katie had died, along with a local boy named Thomas, in a car accident about a year ago. It was a dark night and raining hard. The road was very slippery. Thomas lost control of his car, and it slid into a tree. Both Thomas and Katie were killed instantly.

Jacob was quiet. "So, you see," I said. "I can't disappoint my parents. They had two sons, but both died when they were babies. Katie and I were all they had. And now, I'm the only one left."

"And you're saying it would disappoint them if you were in love with me?" Jacob asked.

"It's not you, Jacob. It would disappoint them if I were romantically interested in anyone who was not part of our community and our church." I couldn't think of any other way to explain it.

The rest blurs together. We eventually went outside to check if there was any damage to Father's car. The boys' father had parked the car beside the cottage. There were scratches from the bicycle I hit but nothing serious. Luckily, the car is large and sturdy and so old that a few more scratches on the bumper will not worry Father. Jacob kept asking me to stay longer, to eat dinner with him, but it was time for me to go.

Before I left, I told Jacob how much I valued him and our friendship. And I explained what it had cost me to tell him about Katie. He said he understood and was glad that I knew I could trust him.

Jacob said he would reciprocate. He would tell me a guarded secret that was difficult to say aloud. He told me everyone in his family had been killed in Poland during the war. But then he stopped. He could go no further. Tears ran down his face, but no sound came out of his mouth. I wanted to help him.

"Write," I said. "If you cannot say the words, write them down." I told him how writing in my diary has helped me cope with my pain and that I believed when he found the right words to release his memories, they wouldn't have so much power over him. Then he would feel better, too.

He said he would feel foolish writing to himself, so I told him to write letters to me, to pretend he was talking to me. Jacob reluctantly agreed. He said he would do anything for me.

When I returned home, I ate little of Mother's dinner and said little to my parents. I had to keep everything inside me until I could write it all down. I couldn't wait to sit down at this desk, grab a pen and my diary, and record everything that happened today.

I still am angry with Cousin Mary. But to be fair, I don't regret today. I think I like Jacob Friedman far more than I should!

Tomorrow I will have to ask Father if I bear any responsibility for the Weaver boy's damaged bicycle. I almost forgot about that.

CHAPTER 25

"WELL, NOW WE know why and when Anna convinced Jacob to write letters to her," Sarah said.

"Jacob wrote that he quickly fell in love with Anna. Now we also know that just a short time later, Anna began falling for him, too," Paula said. "You've got to love a good romance. Right, Ellen?"

Ellen sighed. "It's hard to think of my father with another woman. However, the man who fell in love with Anna was sensitive and emotional, not at all like the dad I knew. I often feel that the Jacob who wrote these letters was really not my father but a completely different person. And then, there are things that remind me so much of my dad that I'm sure this Jacob Friedman could be nobody else. I can easily visualize my father making dinner for Anna and serving her *rugelach*. My father used to bake *rugelach* for me. My dad loved to cook. My mother and I were often commandeered to help, but he was the chef in charge of our kitchen. Yes, he would have baked and cooked for Anna. That is the way he expressed himself, not with words but with food."

"What about that cottage filled with books?" Paula asked. "Ellen, did your father ever tell you about that?"

"No, not a word," Ellen said. "But that he would live in such a place doesn't surprise me. My dad loved books. Our house was filled with them, and he always treated his books with great care. In fact, when I was a child, I always thought he loved them more than he loved me."

"I remember there was a quaint bookstore downtown. It was called Friedman's Book Nook. Was that your father's store?" Sarah asked.

"Yes," Ellen said. "I loved going there when I was little, especially when the store was closed. My dad would do his paperwork, and I would have the run of the place. Mostly, I stayed in the children's section. I would build a fort out of books and sit in the middle of it and read. I loved that."

"Did your father ever tell you he had once been a kosher butcher?" Paula asked.

"No, that was a surprise. I hope he explains when and why he changed professions in one of his letters," Ellen said.

"We did learn in this entry about Anna's sister's death. I bet that was the accident Anna referred to earlier," Sarah said. "That's the kind of loss that would cause a person to turn inward, shy away from friends and seek solace in a diary. But we still haven't learned why Jacob was wearing a dented bullet on a chain when Anna met him."

"That's true. Maybe it will be mentioned in the next letter. Let's keep going. I'm anxious to find out what happened to my father after he escaped Treblinka. Where did he go? What did he do?"

Sarah said, "I skimmed Letter 7. I think it will answer some of your questions, Ellen. I'll find it and read it aloud."

CHAPTER 26

Dearest Anna,

I have shared a lot with you in these letters, but you haven't read my words. When you do, will you pity me for what I have been through, for what I have lost? I don't want that. I want to start living again, fresh and clean. I want to start over again with you. You want to know me, know my past. Do I have to have a past? Can't I just be the new Jacob, the man who lives freely in America and loves you? Isn't that enough?

In my last letter, I described how I escaped from Treblinka and ended up in a forest. I ran, walked, and stumbled through the woods until I was exhausted. I didn't know where I was going. My only goal was to get as far away from Treblinka as I could. I fell into a ditch and covered myself with some leaves and branches and slept there for a while. Afterwards, I pushed on. I was very thirsty. When I heard running water, I followed it and found a stream.

That's where I met Shlomo, crouched over, splashing water on his face. At first I thought that Shlomo was a small person, but I realized when he stood up that he was really a tall thin boy, a Jewish teenager who had a hunting rifle slung over his shoulder and a surly expression on his handsome face. Shlomo was angry. The uprising had poured scores of Jews into the forest followed by a horde of Germans. Shlomo was the leader of a small group of Jewish partisans. He did not appreciate the fact that the big escape from Treblinka had focused attention on the very spot where he was hiding with his followers. His group could not support a massive influx of weak, sick Jews. They needed fighters and weapons to attack the Germans, not more obstacles thrown in their path. He was upset that no one had gotten word to him about the rebellion and the fact that the Germans would literally be beating the bushes to find Jews in the forest.

You see, Shlomo had been caught with his pants down when the explosions went off in Treblinka. Yes, Anna, I mean this literally. His pants were around his ankles at the time. He had been foraging for food and had encountered a sympathetic and lonely farmer's wife. Shlomo had wooed her into a tryst in a haystack, and the escape had interrupted his romantic fling.

I hope I am not embarrassing you, Anna, but even a war cannot control a boy's "raging hormones." Shlomo thought of himself as a magnet for Polish ladies whose soldier husbands were fighting far from home. Shlomo believed he had two missions in life, to kill Germans and to make love to as many women as he could before he died.

Now, I will tell you something you might find hard to believe, Anna. I, Jacob Friedman, became a freedom fighter. I had never been a fighter of any sort, but I joined Shlomo's gang. I didn't know what else to do. I didn't have anywhere else to go. The members of Shlomo's gang had fought in the Warsaw ghetto uprising. A Polish underground group had helped them escape the ghetto before the Germans sent the last trainloads of Jews to Treblinka. However, even among the freedom fighters, there were anti-Semitic factions, so Shlomo and his eight followers broke away to fight Germans on their own. Shlomo was reluctant to let me join his group. He saw me as a liability, someone who would slow his fighters down and need to be cared for. So, I set out to prove myself worthy of membership. Even though I was tired and hungry when I met Shlomo, I kept up with him as he moved quickly through the forest. He led me to a narrow cave that was cleverly concealed by interwoven tree limbs. That's where Shlomo's fighters hid. I cooked for them, made myself useful, and was accepted by the group.

I was with Shlomo's gang about a year. There were some lively arguments around the campfire every night. Leon, a very Orthodox Jew, had no qualms about helping God and killing German soldiers to end the war, but he was very upset with the Zionists who wanted to make Palestine a Jewish state. He adamantly felt that only God had the right to do such a thing in His own time. In response to this, Shlomo would shout and gesture wildly. When the war ended, Shlomo wanted to go to Palestine, join the Zionists, and fight for a Jewish state. He argued that Jews had to have a safe homeland because they had no homes to return to, and it had to be Israel, the land God promised them. Shlomo repeatedly uttered the words "never again!"

I hated the Germans for what they had done. I also hated the Germans for turning me into someone I didn't want to be, a man who shot with the intent to kill. I don't know if I personally killed any Germans as my hands always shook whenever I handled a gun. I promised myself if I lived through the war, I would never pick up a gun again. I dreamed of living in a quiet place that had bookstores and libraries. I missed reading very much, even more than I missed food!

It was typhus that put an end to my life as a guerrilla fighter. Anna, the disease killed so many in the Warsaw ghetto and in Treblinka. In those crowded, unsanitary places body lice enjoyed a veritable human feast. When the people scratched at their bites, they often infected their wounds with the feces from the lice and came down with typhus. It's a terrible disease that spreads like wildfire. There were many rats in the forest, too. Rats can carry the infection, and when fleas bite the rats, the fleas also become carriers. I was always dirty when I lived in the forest, so it was not surprising I became infected.

Shortly after my friend Leon developed a high fever and a rash on his chest, I did, too. We both had muscle aches and chills, and I was alarmed when our rashes began to spread to our backs, stomachs, arms, and legs. I knew we had typhus. Before too long, Leon and I were too weak to keep up with the group.

Shlomo had no choice. He dropped us off at a school maintained by an order of nuns. Word had spread among the underground fighters that these nuns would sometimes help Jews. Shlomo told us that he was sorry he had to leave us behind. The nuns were kind and did the best they could with the limited medicines they had on hand. The hid us beneath some painting tarps in a storage room, and after a few days of rest and a little food, we were strong enough to be moved to a nearby farm.

We couldn't stay with the nuns. They had taken in many Jewish children. To pass the children off as Catholic orphans, the sisters had obtained false papers for them, including phony baptismal certificates. The nuns had already put themselves at great risk for the Jewish children in their care. In Nazi Poland when someone was caught helping or sheltering a Jew, not only was that person killed, but all the members in that person's family were killed, too. If we had been found at

the school, the Germans would have killed all the nuns and
burned the school to the ground. With so much at stake, we
had to leave. The nuns persuaded a local farmer to hide us in
the loft of his barn.

The farmer came to the school. He had mounds of hay
in his wagon. He created a small space for Leon and me in
the center, threw a blanket over us, and covered us with hay.
It was so hard to breathe, and the dust from the hay was so
thick I could taste it. It was a miserable ride to the farm. Our
muscles ached from the typhus. The road was rocky, and
every bounce sent jolts of pain through us. It seemed to take
forever, but, actually, we had not gone that far. At one point,
shortly before we reached the farm, two German soldiers
stopped the farmer. We heard the farmer's horse neigh and
impatiently paw the ground. One soldier walked around the
wagon, randomly jabbing at the hay with his rifle, while the
other spoke to the farmer.

I thought, "This is how it ends. I have only a few minutes
left to live." Leon must have been frightened, too; I felt his
body shake beside mine. Then, I heard a good sound. The
farmer was laughing. He was joking with the soldiers. He was
playfully arguing with them, too. The soldiers wanted to buy
three bottles of liquor from his still for a very low price, and
he was insisting they pay him more. After a bit of haggling,
they settled on an agreeable sum. The soldiers said they would
stop by the farm later to get their liquor. I was so relieved
when I heard the farmer make a clucking sound. Thank
goodness, his horse responded and moved forward again.

The nuns had told us that this farmer named Jan, a wily
fellow in his seventies, was honorable and generous, but I
found out later he really was just hedging his bets. It was
August of 1944. He knew the Russians were moving towards
his town and hoped this charitable act would save him if the
Allies won the war and found out he had been doing business

with the Germans. In addition, he was confident he had a foolproof place to stash us for a short time.

Jan had a storage space in the loft of his barn. It was filled with broken furniture and crates. On one side, there was a large unit filled with tools. This storage piece was immense, stretching from the floor of the loft to the sloped ceiling. Because the unit was so tall and so wide, it was positioned at an angle, and a bit of unusable space was hidden directly behind it. The farmer, an accomplished carpenter, put small hinges on the boards behind the bottom shelf. The distance between the bottom shelf and the next shelf was almost three feet. When the boards swung open, a man could crawl into the hiding place behind the shelving unit. There wasn't much room behind this storage piece, just enough for two pallets, a water pitcher, and a chamber pot. Anna, this is where Leon and I hid.

Because the barn had a sloped roof, we couldn't stand fully upright there. So, every once in a while, despite the fact Jan warned us not to, one of us would act as a look-out while the other went through the opening in the storage unit and walked around the loft. We feared if we didn't stretch our backs and move our legs, we wouldn't be able to walk when we were finally released.

The barn was old and poorly built. From our hiding place, we could easily see the farmhouse and yard through the many crevices between the boards. That is how we kept track of the comings and goings of Jan, his wife Maria, and Jan's customers. Those many small openings were our only light source. Still, I often cursed them. Everything came through them: sun, wind, rain, insects, and snow. We baked in the summer and froze in the winter.

Initially, Jan and Maria were friendly and helpful. During August, Leon and I were both weak from typhus, limp from the heat, and, I admit, very docile. Jan and Maria tried to make us as comfortable as they could. It took a long time for us to regain our strength.

Meanwhile, local Polish citizens and underground fighters rallied and tried to regain control of Warsaw before the Soviet army marched into the city. Jan was confident his countrymen would win the battle for Warsaw in a few days. He relayed optimistic reports. Soon, he told us, the Soviets would join the fight and chase the Germans out of Poland. Soon, he claimed, it would be safe for us to leave the barn.

Leon and I were so bored, trapped in a small space with nothing to do. So, we passed the time by telling each other stories. We shared everything, stories about our families, hometowns, friends, and acquaintances. When we ran out of tales about places we had visited and people we knew, we talked about books we had read. Oh, how I yearned for a book to read! Jan had only one book, his family's Bible, but he wouldn't share it with us. He said it was his family's only heirloom and did not belong in a dirty barn. So, Leon and I discussed politics, religion, and philosophy. We argued when our ideas differed and laughed companionably when we discovered we agreed. Hours and hours of talk, and still there was time left. Then, we made up word games, and we made up stories. We talked on and on while we waited for the war to end.

Leon became my brother. Anna, I have never before or since told anyone so much about myself. All we did in the loft was sleep, talk, and eat. Maria and Jan took turns bringing us food twice a day. It was never much, but I think my stomach had shrunk in Treblinka. I was so grateful for the watery soup and the slice of dark bread, our daily staples. I liked it better when Jan came with our meals. He would stay for a few minutes and talk to us about the war. We were starved for information and lived on his tidbits of news for days.

103

At first, his wife Maria would smile at us when she delivered our meals; she was missing quite a few teeth. She had a wrinkled face, thin gray hair, and a short bulky body. However, over time, we saw her smile less and less. She would purse her lips and shake her head. She told us she was angry with her husband for hiding troublesome Jews.

As the weeks passed, the number of German soldiers stopping by the farm increased. Some came, as usual, to buy liquor, but there were also many, headed towards the fight in Warsaw, who came looking for food. Jan feared the German soldiers would confiscate Henryk, his old horse. He hid Henryk in the forest during the day. Late one afternoon, we had a scare when some soldiers pounded up the ladder to the loft. We heard Jan and Maria loudly protesting, yelling over and over that they did not have any food hidden in the barn. The soldiers poked around a bit and overturned some crates. They actually pushed on the heavy storage unit. Luckily, it did not budge. The soldiers swore loudly and complained that there was nothing of value to steal. Leon and I sighed with relief when they left the barn. We both had been very frightened.

After that incident, Maria looked at us with disgust. She said little after that. She wanted us gone. She muttered that we were putting her and Jan in danger. She would wave a stubby finger at us and say, "Don't even think about leaving. You can't go now." More Germans were at checkpoints and patrolling the roads. She feared we would be captured, tortured for information, and, before we died, made to reveal who had given us shelter and aid. She hated us for being in the loft. She also hated the fact that there wasn't a safe way to get rid of us.

The Warsaw uprising lasted for several months and ended poorly for the Poles and for us, too. The Germans were the victors and still in control of the area. Leon and I grew

104

restless; we were feeling better, and we were anxious to move out of our cramped hiding spot and rejoin Shlomo's group. Anna, you can't imagine our disappointment when Jan told us that Shlomo and the other partisans had either been killed fighting for Warsaw or had left the area to regroup. We had nowhere to go; we were stuck. We had to wait for the Soviet army to liberate this section of Poland.

Maria became surlier when Warsaw fell. She was angry with the Germans for killing so many Poles and burning a good portion of the city. "What are the Allied forces waiting for?" she would demand of us, as if we were privy to the Allied leaders' thoughts from our place in the loft. By mid-November, she stopped talking to us, and, I noticed, our food portions dramatically declined when she brought our meals. We got substantially more when it was Jan's turn. It was very cold in December, and Maria developed a deep rumbling cough. When we saw her, she would sniffle and sneeze and press a dirty handkerchief to her mouth. She looked very pale and shaky.

I was worried about Leon when he started to cough, too. Cold winds whistled through the barn and made us both shiver. We each had one thin blanket. That's all we had to keep us warm. I tried to plug up the many holes between the boards with scraps of hay mixed with our waste and horse manure. It was not the most sanitary solution, but it helped. The horse, Henryk, was the only animal left in the barn. All the other farm animals had been eaten by Jan and Maria, traded for goods, or stolen by the Germans. Sometimes, in the middle of the night when I snuck down from the loft to gather bits of the horse's hay and some of its dung, I would hug the mangy, swaybacked animal and try to draw some of its warmth into my bones. I was so cold! Leon prayed all the time for the war to finally end; I had given up on God, but Leon clung to the hope He would hear his prayer. I didn't

have the heart to argue with Leon about God. Leon was a true
believer. Saying the traditional prayers comforted him.

One morning in the middle of December, there was a lot
of activity in the yard. All day long, people visited Jan's house,
not soldiers but peasants dressed in dark clothes. Leon and
I spent the day trying to figure out what was going on. We
guessed something might have happened to Maria; she looked
terribly ill when we last saw her. We waited, but neither Jan
nor Maria brought us any food. It was a long cold day. We
didn't know if it was best to stay in our hiding place or to
run away. I was worried about Leon. He was feverish, and
his cough was much worse. His body shook when he tried to
muffle the sounds of his growling coughs. I didn't think he
could survive out in the open. There was snow on the ground,
and the winds were strong. I didn't know if I had the strength
to carry Leon if he should collapse. So, we waited. Although
Leon begged me to run away and save myself, there was no
way I was going to leave without him. Whatever fate would
bring us, we would face it together.

Finally, late that night, we heard the sound of the barn
door opening and heard Jan's voice as he greeted Henryk, his
horse. When he entered the hiding place, Jan had a small sack
of food with him and a bottle of fresh water. He apologized
for not coming sooner. He bowed his head. I could see he was
trying to gain control of his emotions. His eyes were rimmed
in red and bloodshot. Jan's words came out in a blubbery
rush. Maria had died. She was laid out in her Sunday best in
a coffin in their front room. She would be buried the next day
in the little cemetery next to their church.

Jan told us to try to make the food in the sack last as long
as we could. He said he would eventually return with more;
however, with friends and family visiting again tomorrow, it
would be difficult for him to slip away without being noticed
until late at night. I clasped his hands and gave them a

sympathetic squeeze. Leon and I both told him how sorry we were that Maria had died and that we would never forget the sacrifices the two of them had made for us. We owed them our lives.

After Jan left us, Leon and I fell into a fitful sleep. We were so cold. Jan had said nothing about the war. Would it ever end? In the morning, Leon was much worse. His teeth were chattering so much I feared he would wear them down to small nubs. His forehead felt hot when I touched it. I crawled out of our space and fumbled about in the loft, searching for something to cover Leon to keep him warm. I didn't find anything. Although I heard heavy footsteps in the yard outside the barn, I climbed down the ladder from the loft. I couldn't believe what I saw, a blanket. Last night when he delivered our food, Jan must have tossed a blanket on Henryk to keep his horse warm. I patted the animal's side, quietly asked the gentle beast to forgive me, and stole the blanket. When I returned to our hiding place, I tried to share my body heat with Leon. I wrapped us both up in our blankets and Henryk's, too.

At first, I was grateful when Leon stopped coughing and fell asleep. I was scared someone in the yard would hear his loud reverberating coughs. Sleep, I thought, was good for him. He would rest and regain his strength. Surely, under the circumstances, without hot soup or helpful medicines, sleep is what he needed most. But, several hours later, I became concerned. Leon felt so cold, and I could not rouse him. I shook him and shook him, and still he did not wake.

"Wake up now, Leon,'" I whispered. "Talk to me. We are in this together, my friend. Don't die. Don't leave me here all alone."

But Leon did not wake. He did not respond. His body felt very cold.

"Please, God," I cried, forgetting that I no longer believed in God and not caring if my voice was heard. "Please help Leon. He's a good man. Please!"

But God ignored my plea as He ignored all my prayers. Leon's body was cold and stiff. Leon, like everyone else I loved, was dead.

Anna, you would think after all the deaths I saw that one more would not hurt so much. But it did. It hurt very much. It still hurts.

That is all I can write tonight.

Love,

Jacob

CHAPTER 27

"I REMEMBER THE name Leon. It was mentioned in one of the diary entries I worked on," Paula said.

Paula shuffled through one of the piles on the dining room table, found the papers she was hunting for, and began to read aloud.

༄

Friday, October 10, 1947

It is getting colder. I wore my thickest sweater to the library today, and I brought along a thermos of hot coffee, too. It soon will be too cold for Jacob and me to sit outside the library on "our" bench and talk. Does this worry Jacob?

Jacob was unusually quiet when we met today. When I asked him if anything was wrong, he told me that last night he wrote me a letter, a long letter, and now he felt drained. I asked him if he felt better now or worse. He said he wasn't sure. He told me that he had been writing letters to me about his war experiences, and now he was curious to learn what was in the World War II book I had read. I told Jacob that the book is a compilation of the letters a local soldier wrote to his sister during the war. It is divided into three parts. In the first set of letters, the soldier explains why, after much soul searching, he decided to enlist as a Conscientious Objector. In the next set, he describes how he treated wounded soldiers after he became a medic. In the third group, he writes about the liberation of Buchenwald, a concentration camp in Germany. He describes what he saw in horrific detail, the skeletal people and the mounds of dead bodies. Jacob stared off in the distance as I rambled on a bit more.

Jacob nodded. "He told the truth. I can't believe it. He was allowed to tell the truth." Jacob was so surprised. Then, Jacob reached for my hand and squeezed it gently. He said he couldn't tell me everything he had written in his letters, but he would share a little. He told me that he had been in the Warsaw ghetto with his wife and daughter before they were shipped off to Treblinka, a death camp. His family was killed there. After Jacob escaped from Treblinka, he hid with his friend Leon in a barn in Poland, and Leon died, too. Jacob explained that he had written about Leon's death last night and reliving that time had been exceedingly difficult for him. Jacob said, "I don't know why I didn't die. There were so many opportunities for me to die. I don't know why I'm alive. Maybe I was spared so I could meet you."

I slid closer to Jacob and hugged him. I didn't think about it. I just did it. He hugged me back hard, and I felt his tears falling on my neck. I started to cry, too. We stayed that way for a long time, clinging to each other, and then I heard the backdoor of the library opening, and I pulled away.

I felt like I did when I was thrown off a horse, shocked and hurt. I was upset because I hadn't known that Jacob had been through such tragedies, upset because I had no idea he had been married and had a child, and upset because I had almost been caught embracing a man in public. I'm shallow and selfish, worrying about myself at a time like that.

We were distracted by a mother, carrying an armful of books, who had opened the library's back door, and we silently waited until she and her two small children left the area.

Jacob wiped his eyes with a handkerchief and then thanked me again for bringing coffee. He said he had a surprise for me and asked me to please follow him. I realized that Jacob had shifted gears, and I knew the intimacy of the embrace had ended. I was relieved and disappointed. Oh, probably more disappointed but still relieved. I followed Jacob. He walked briskly through the library and out the front door to the sidewalk in front of the building. He turned to the right and walked past one shop but then stopped at the next and grinned.

"Here it is," Jacob said. "Our new meeting place. It will be warm and very proper."

I told Jacob that meeting in front of a store on a busy street would be neither warm nor proper.

Jacob laughed. The store had a "Closed" sign in the window, but Jacob magically pulled a key out of his pocket and opened the door. It was a cafe with chairs around small circular tables. Jacob explained that last week, as he was leaving the library, he had met the new owner of the cafe and then had "auditioned" for a position as a part-time pastry chef. Now he would be baking for the weekend crowds. But what was most important, the cafe was closed on Friday afternoons. We would now have a warm private place, close to the library, to meet through the fall and winter, but it would also be a proper place. We would be chaperoned. I could hear muted sounds from the kitchen and knew people were cooking and washing dishes back there.

So, Jacob was thinking ahead. Jacob was thinking of me. Too much time had passed. I had to get back to the market. Before I left, I asked Jacob when I would be able to read the letters he had written to me.

"Not now," he said, "but, hopefully, soon. Before we marry."

I didn't know what to say. There wasn't time to respond. I blushed. I touched my cheek, and it was hot. I hurried back to the market. I was late, and Father was not pleased.

CHAPTER 28

"Now things are progressing," Sarah said. "Their first hug."

"Yes," Ellen said, "I am curious about their romance, too, but I hope you both will forgive me. I know it's irrational, but I will feel a lot better when we get my father out of the war. Did either of you read what happened to my dad after Leon died in their hiding place?"

"I did," Sarah said. "Letter 8 starts with burying Leon, but I didn't get a chance to finish skimming it before we stopped for lunch. I don't know where it will lead us, but there is only one way to find out. I'll read it aloud now."

⋅◦⦿◦⋅

Letter 8

Dearest Anna,

I will complete the story. I will tell you in this letter what happened after Leon died. I will squeeze out the last drips of my pain, and then you can judge if there is anything left of me that is worth salvaging.

I helped Jan dig a shallow grave for Leon in the barn. We put Henryk's water trough over the spot; it hid the place where we had disturbed the earth floor. I stayed in the loft, and Jan continued to bring me food and water. I felt light-headed and feverish. I started to cough, too. I was sick. I thought I would surely die. I don't know why I didn't.

I was in the hiding place for a total of six months. One morning Jan very matter-of-factly said, "It's time to go. The Soviets have liberated Auschwitz. I will take you there. Someone will take care of you there."

I only vaguely remember the ride. Jan helped me climb into his wagon. He covered me with blankets; this time not to hide me but to keep me warm. I remember mumbling some words of thanks to Jan when he left me with a Soviet soldier. Jan patted me on the back before he left. I recall other images from that time. There was a big burly man with a black beard in a white coat. He always smelled of garlic. I think he must have been a doctor. He had kind dark eyes and a scar across his forehead. That is all I remember about him. I slept, sipped some watery soup, and drank some foul-tasting concoction that soothed my throat and helped me stop coughing. Eventually, I felt better.

I joined a group of Jewish refugees. We wandered around a bit. There were so many people moving from one displaced persons' camp to another, thousands following rumors. Some were looking for lost relatives and friends. Some were searching for the quickest way to get to Palestine or the United States. I didn't know what I wanted. It was just easier to let others make decisions for me, to move when the group moved and stop when it stopped. In every town and camp, I found myself looking over the posted lists of survivors and searching, searching for the name of someone from my hometown. I was searching for the name of a family member, no matter how distantly related, who survived. I was still alive. There had to be someone I knew before the war who was alive as well.

I ended up in Foehrenwald, the large, displaced persons' camp in the American zone southwest of Munich. There were over four thousand refugees there when I arrived. I remember the first night I was in the camp I collapsed in exhaustion in a crowded tent. I was so tired. I thought, "Enough with this wandering around. Maybe I should just go back to my hometown in Poland, back to Kaluszyn, and see for myself what is left." I knew why I hadn't done this. I was afraid there would be nothing left. I groaned. I felt empty, very empty.

I was annoyed when I felt my leg being repeatedly hit by something. I heard someone say, "You, wake up now and move!" I sat up, prepared to give a good tongue lashing to whoever was disturbing me. I was too tired to give up my sleeping place to another. I was entitled to it just as much as anyone else.

You can't imagine my surprise, Anna, when I realized that the man hitting my leg with his crutch was Joseph Federman. I knew Joseph Federman! He was from Kaluszyn! Joseph had been *bar mitzvahed* two years ahead of me. We had studied at the same school. I hadn't known him well, and I didn't particularly like what I knew. Joseph's family was well-to-do, and he had grown up into a demanding, spoiled bully. I had learned it was best to stay out of his way. He enjoyed taunting and hitting smaller, younger boys. And here he was. An older thinner version of himself, but he still was Joseph Federman from Kaluszyn. I started to laugh in relief; someone I knew was still alive! We hugged and whooped for joy. People in the tent shouted at us, told us to be quiet. Joseph and I left the tent to talk.

Well, Anna, we talked and talked. I learned that when I moved to Warsaw with Esther and Rachel that Joseph had used his money and connections to get his family out of Poland and settled in Amsterdam. Still, despite his foresight and careful planning, we both ended up in the same place,

Foehrenwald. We both had lost our wives and children. Then, I asked Joseph about our home, about Kaluszyn. What he said chilled me to the bone.

Joseph went back to Kaluszyn. He didn't know where else to go. He thought everyone would rejoice and marvel at the fact that he survived. But when he went back, there were no Jews. The synagogue and many of the Jewish homes were just rubble. He went to his home. It was the nicest in our neighborhood, and a Polish family was living in it. He told them that they were living in his house. The mother and children glared at him suspiciously. They said they didn't believe him. The father said it wasn't fair. Why should his family move out of the house when their neighbors could keep the Jewish homes they had taken? Why should they suffer? Joseph was insistent and told them the house was all he had. He had no idea if he would ever see the money he had left in the bank. The father pointed a rifle at his chest and ordered him to leave. Joseph was shocked and stood rooted to the ground. A bullet whizzed past his ear and another bounced off the ground near his feet. He turned and ran but not before a bullet nicked his leg. The father yelled obscenities at him as he fled, said he would kill Joseph if he ever returned and that no one would care about one more dead Jew.

Joseph said, "Don't go back, Jacob. There is nothing left for us there. We can't go home."

That settled things for me. I would not go back. I did not want to live in a hostile place where I would constantly be haunted by ghosts and memories. So, I, like so many others, applied for an entry visa to the United States. I waited in the camp, and the days passed slowly. Joseph stayed by my side. The bully from my childhood had become an engaging and funny man. Many found his gallows humor twisted and shocking, but I enjoyed it. It kept me from thinking about the past and worrying about the future. Joseph moved around well with the help of his crutch, but I noticed he often winced in pain. He showed me the bullet a doctor had removed from his upper thigh. At Foehrenwald, he talked a dentist into drilling a hole in it for him. He kept the bullet close to his heart; it dangled from a string he wore around his neck. I thought it was a very peculiar necklace, but Joseph liked it. He said the Germans and Poles had taken so much from him. They left him with only his life and that bullet and that he planned on keeping both! That was so typical of Joseph.

Joseph had cousins in New York City, and he wrote to them, begging them to sponsor his immigration to America and to consider helping his good friend Jacob, too. I remember how excited I was every time he received a letter from the United States. Each time we hoped it would contain the travel papers that would enable him to leave the camp and go to America.

I was in Foehrenwald for a year and a half. Joseph and I attended English language classes. We wanted to be ready for our new lives in America. We avidly followed all the news reports about immigration and quotas. We waited and waited for the United States to grant us entry visas.

In the meantime, many of the young Jewish men and women in the camp were marrying and having children to replace some of the lives that were lost. Anna, Jews usually name their babies after deceased relatives they want to honor and remember. So, there was a baby boom in the camp, and people had no shortage of names to choose from.

I met a lovely tall woman named Judith at the camp, and for a while I thought I might marry her. But it didn't feel right. I wasn't ready. When I held Judith in my arms, all I could think about was Esther. I felt like a married man who was cheating on his wife. I pulled away in shame, and Judith moved on and married another man.

Months later, I found myself attracted to Devorah, a tiny woman with a head of curly red hair and a big throaty laugh. She was brash and confident enough for the two of us. She was so different from Esther that I thought it might work. However, when a man named Nachum wooed her away from me, I was sad and my ego was hurt, but I was not devastated by the loss. I knew then that Devorah had been a pleasant diversion, but I did not love her with all my heart. Not the way I had loved Esther. Not the way I love you, Anna.

One morning I heard that a volunteer from the American Jewish Joint Distribution Committee was looking for Joseph. Workers from "The Joint" were angels who helped Jewish refugees. This volunteer was a middle-aged woman with a strong New York accent who wore thick glasses. She had a large envelope for Joseph that had been mailed from the United States. I found the woman, grabbed her by the hand, and hurriedly pulled her over to the infirmary.

"Here," I said to the lady and pointed to Joseph who was lying on a cot and coughing. "Here he is. If there is good news in that envelope, it will be better for him than any medicine."

Joseph tore open the envelope, and a ticket for passage on a ship and official papers fell out of it. He gasped in astonishment. I'm ashamed to admit that while I tried to look excited and happy for him, I was sad, too. My friend was going to America while I would remain indefinitely in the camp.

"Don't worry, Jacob," Joseph said. "I will get a job in America and help you get a visa, too. I promise."

And I knew he meant it. He had become a very good friend. But Joseph never got the chance to fulfill his promise. There was a tuberculosis epidemic in the camp that summer, the summer of 1946, and hundreds died. Joseph was one of them. Initially, I thought he just had an awfully bad cold and nagging cough. I had to face the severity of his illness when he began to cough up blood. I remember when the lady with the thick glasses from "The Joint" came back to see me I was still grieving for my friend. She said she had a great idea. She spoke, but the words only partially registered in my brain.

"Similar names. Same hometown. Small changes. Use ticket," I repeated the words I had absorbed.

"Yes, yes," she said. "It will work. We can't let a good visa and boat ticket go to waste. You can do it. Jacob Friedman can become Joseph Federman."

"But what will Joseph's cousins say? They don't know me. They sent everything for him, not for me."

She said, "I'll write to them. I'll explain everything. I'll tell them all about you. I'll tell them that Joseph was your good friend. I'll get them to agree. It will work. Wait and see. It will work!"

And that, Anna, is how I came to America, courtesy of my friend Joseph Federman and his generous cousins. And that, Anna, is why I wear this dented bullet on a chain around my neck. It's the bullet that was in Joseph's leg. He gave it to me the day before he died. I wear it because it was important to Joseph. I'll never forget Joseph and all he did for me.

It's late. I'll stop here and go to bed. If I'm lucky, I'll dream of you. Anna, do you ever dream of me?

Love,

Jacob

CHAPTER 29

"THE DENTED BULLET," said Paula. "Now we know why Jacob was wearing a dented bullet when he met Anna."

"But," Ellen said, "I never saw my father wear such a thing. Believe me, I would have remembered. At some point, he stopped. I wonder when and why."

Sarah said, "It's amazing. We answer one question, but it leads us to more."

"Well," Ellen said as she stretched her arms above her head. "We've covered a lot. I think it's time for a break. Agreed? How about a snack? We can pop some popcorn."

"Now, that's a great idea," Sarah said, and Paula nodded in agreement.

⚬

A short time later the three writing buddies were comfortably ensconced in Ellen's family room. Ellen had settled into her favorite recliner, Paula was sprawled out on the couch, and Sarah had appropriated two plush pillows for her head and was stretched out in front of the fireplace. Each had a bowl perched on her lap and was contentedly munching buttery kernels of popcorn.

Paula was the first to break the silence. "Jacob was born in 1920. Therefore, he was twenty-seven years old in 1947 when he met Anna. He had married, born a child, lost a family and been through a war. He experienced a lot in a short time. Meanwhile, Anna had been living a quiet life with her family in Pennsylvania. Cousin Mary chided Anna about being twenty years old and unmarried. By today's standards, both were young, people who would be in college or just starting their careers, and, perhaps, turning to online dating services to meet the right mate."

Sarah said, "I wonder if Anna ever took part in a Walk-a-Mile."

"What's that?" Ellen asked.

Sarah said, "Well, there were prohibitions against dancing, TV, and movies in many Mennonite churches, so young people couldn't date the way others did. Instead, on Sunday nights they would find a quiet rural road. Girls would form a single line, and the boys would stand in a line beside them. If the church allowed it, they would hold hands. They would walk and talk to each other until one boy would tap the shoulder of the boy in front of him, and then the boys would all move up one slot to talk to another girl. It's the Mennonite version of speed dating."

"Did it work for your parents?" Paula asked.

"No," Sarah said and then grinned. "My mom was a rebel. She dated a boy when she was fifteen years old. Her behavior was scandalous because she didn't wait until she was Sweet Sixteen to start dating. However, it all ended well. Right after her high school graduation, my mother married my father, her one and only boyfriend, and they're still happily married today."

"I must admit that I like those kind of love stories," Paula said. "True and lasting love. That's what I'm looking for, and maybe it's why I write romance tales. Right now, I'm searching for a special Prince Charming. Actually, he must be more than just charming. Charming just skims the surface, and I need more. I want a guy who's gentle, funny, and smart. And one who will stay through thick and through thin. After all I've been through with my marriage and divorce, I want a really good man. I refuse to settle for less."

"You haven't said very much about your ex-husband. Is he a good father to the boys?" Ellen asked.

"Unfortunately, I married a boy and not a man. Everything was great when it was just the two of us, but then it all changed after we had children. I hadn't realized how much I had been mothering Ron. I was so exhausted after the twins were born and upset because Ron was no help at all. It was easier when he wasn't at home because then I could concentrate on the babies and not have to care for Ron, too. We weren't planning on having any more children. Our New York apartment was so small. There was barely room for the four of us, and then I was pregnant with our third son. Ron blamed me, conveniently forgetting that he was responsible, too. He was home less and less after that, and, quite honestly, I minded less and less. We stayed together for the boys, but last year Ron said he found the love of his life and wanted out. Here's the strange thing. The woman he left me for has two little girls of her own. I don't get it. Does he really expect things to be different? But I knew there was nothing left to fight for, so I was happy to get out of the marriage. Since I moved to Lancaster, Ron has only seen the boys a few times. I, frankly, was surprised when he kept his promise and took them this weekend. He helps financially, but the boys know he's not reliable when it comes to spending time with them. And that breaks my heart."

"Well," said Sarah, "I'm glad you ended up in Lancaster, Paula. You can start over here, and you have an advantage. Single men want to meet the pretty new girl in town. I struggle with dating because I've grown up here and have exhausted so many prospects. And I don't send out the right signals. I don't make the right connections."

"That's hard to believe," said Ellen. "Sarah, you're sensitive and kind. We know that from your writings. And you're so open and friendly."

"Maybe around you two," Sarah said. "But around guys, I'm shy, and I always fall for selfish men who won't make a commitment. I think I can help them and change them, and I give them countless chances. I know I should drop them and move on, but I don't. My sister is so upset with me. She says I'm in this rut because I don't think a really good guy will like me, so I go after the losers. She may be right, but why would a good guy choose me? I have nothing to offer. I dropped out of college because I couldn't decide on a major. I was just taking random classes and racking up more debt. And now, I'm older, but I still don't have a direction. I have a job but not a career, and my close friends are married and moving on with their lives. I just don't fit in anywhere."

"Sarah, you fit in perfectly with us," Ellen said. "And give yourself a break. You still have time. I had a lot to figure out before I pursued the right career and was pursued by the right man. When I was in college, I dated a lot of wrong guys, hoping to get a rise out of my dad. And, get this, dad didn't react. When Mark came into my life, what did I do? I pushed him away because I couldn't believe such a fine guy would ever want someone like me. Luckily for me, Mark stayed and wore down my resistance. Yes, Paula is right. Don't settle. Look for someone who is mature and ready to marry. And you don't need a man you have to change. People don't change. You need a great guy who appreciates you and accepts you just the way you are and has staying power. He doesn't have to be perfect, but he does have to be sweet."

Ellen was surprised. This wasn't like her at all. Who was she to be doling out advice to these young women? What did she know about dating now? Had she overstepped? She was embarrassed. Her guests were quiet. Were they thinking over what she said, or were they getting ready to bolt? They had shared their feelings, and Ellen had wanted to reciprocate. If they left now, Ellen knew she would never forgive herself for chasing them away. The day had been an emotional roller coaster ride. Would it end in a crash? Her father did not bring out the best in her. What would she do if her friends abandoned her? Would she blame that on her father, too?

Sarah stood up and set her bowl on the coffee table. "This has been an incredible day," she said.

"Yes, it has," Paula said. "Thank you, Ellen." Paula placed her bowl inside Sarah's and stood up as well.

Ellen knew what was happening. They were signaling that they were ready to leave.

Paula said, "So, let's see if we can complete a nice chunk of work before we break for dinner. We need to find out what brought Jacob to Lancaster. Okay?"

"Yes," Sarah said. "It was a good break, but now I'm ready to roll."

Ellen was relieved. She was wrong. They were staying, and everything was okay. Why was she still so insecure?

Ellen said, "When and why my father moved to Lancaster are explained in Letter 9. I skimmed that letter. I'll find it and read it aloud."

CHAPTER 30

Dearest Anna,

You took your first bite of a bagel today. I knew you would like it. How could you not? You like bread and rolls, and you like doughnuts. So how could you not like bagels? I made some with great care last night just for you. I don't miss New York City, but I do miss bagels. Now that I am baking for the cafe, I will have to ask Sam, the owner, if he'd be willing to add them to the menu. Probably not, but I will ask.

In my last letter, Anna, I told you about my friend Joseph Federman. I met Joseph's cousins, my sponsors, when I arrived in New York. I made them a promise. I would work and earn money to repay them. I would return all the money they had spent to bring me to the United States. It was only fair. Joseph's cousins owned a grocery store in a Jewish neighborhood in The Bronx. I went to work for them as a kosher butcher. This was something I knew how to do. I lived with one of the cousins; however, I spent little time in the apartment. I just slept there. I worked for ten hours in the store every day. The *Shabbat* was the only day I had off. I

attended English language classes at a nearby public school at
night, and, whenever I could, I studied American history at
the library for my citizenship test, too.

Anna, I got lucky. I was able to reclaim my name. A friend
of one of the cousins had an uncle who was able to help me.
I filled out all the necessary legal forms and claimed that
my entry documents had been destroyed in a fire. After my
paperwork was channeled to this uncle's desk, voila! My own
name appeared on the replacement papers. That is how Jacob
Friedman was resurrected, and Joseph Federman was legally
laid to rest. After World War II, the country was flooded with
new immigrants. As I had legal papers, I was never questioned
about them.

I had few expenses, so every month I was able to return
most of my salary to the Federman family. I continue to send
them a little each month, and soon the debt will be paid in
full. I also regularly send a little money to the nuns in Poland
who helped me and Leon. I learned from the good sisters that
Jan, the farmer who hid me, died shortly after the war. As Jan
and Maria had no children, a nephew inherited the farm. I
sent some money to the nephew, too, and I wrote him a long
letter. Anna, would you believe it? The nephew wrote back
and thanked me! He was proud to learn that his uncle had
defied the Germans and helped a fellow Pole. I still have that
letter. I keep it in my Polish cookbook.

Anna, all this was good. I was making money in New
York and sharing it with those who had saved my life, but I
wasn't happy. I was just going through the motions. Working,
eating, studying, and sleeping. And not much sleeping
because I would dream about my family and the war. I didn't
like the dirt and noise of the city. I yearned for the quiet of a
small town. I wanted to see farms, hills, and trees again.

I thought about moving to Israel and attended a couple of
meetings run by Zionists. I needed a change. And then I met

Chaim, who was also a kosher butcher. Chaim was excited. He heard there were jobs for *shohets* at a new kosher chicken plant in Lancaster, Pennsylvania.

"There are openings. They pay very well," Chaim said. He was driving there to apply for a position, and he begged me to come along. I bet, Anna, you can guess the rest. I accompanied Chaim, and I liked the area. I applied for a job and was immediately hired. And while Chaim and the other kosher butchers return to their families in Philadelphia and New York every weekend, I decided to make Lancaster my home. I found a cottage to rent and began filling it with books.

In Lancaster I worked, ate, studied, and slept in a quieter place, but nothing had changed inside me. I was still lonely, empty, and sad.

And then, Anna, I met you. Now, every week, there is a reason to live until Friday because on Friday there is another opportunity to see you. The world is better now, more colorful. It is beautiful because you are beautiful.

Now there is more to life than just earning money to pay off debts. There is you. You are my world. You are my everything! I understand why you need God and religion in your life, but, Anna, all I need is you!

Love,
Jacob

CHAPTER 31

ELLEN CAREFULLY PLACED the letter on the table. She sighed and then said, "Dad wrote about missing New York bagels. They were so special when I was young. When someone in our community went to New York, they brought back New York bagels for everyone. Funny, isn't it? Today bagels are so common, but that wasn't the case when I was growing up. I remember reading somewhere that for a long time only Jews ate bagels. Now, they're a part of the American diet. And it's strange how many of my memories are centered on food. Dad didn't make bagels at home very often, but when he did, it was usually for company or for a birthday surprise. I think that is why I love bagels so much. They always taste like a special treat."

"It's interesting," Sarah said, "how fate can direct our lives. Jacob was considering moving to Israel, and then he met Chaim and ended up here. If he hadn't met Chaim and Chaim hadn't steered him towards Lancaster, then everything might have changed. He wouldn't have met Anna, and he might not have met Ellen's mother. Ellen might be a different person writing mysteries in Israel."

Paula laughed. "If Ellen was, as you say, a different person, how do you know she would still be writing mysteries?"

"Well," Sarah replied, "she would have to if even a tiny part of her was still our Ellen."

Ellen was thinking about her dad and not paying close attention to this fanciful exchange. When he arrived in the United States, her father didn't have family members to care for or to influence his choices. His trade limited where he could work, but at some point, he did change occupations. Was her father in control of his life? Was fate directing him? Was God?

"At the end of this letter," Ellen said, "my father wrote that, unlike Anna, he didn't need God nor religion. I remember a diary entry where Anna wrote about a discussion she had with my dad about religion."

Ellen shuffled through some papers till she found the one she was searching for. "Here it is," she said, and then she read Anna's words aloud.

CHAPTER 32

*It has been pleasant chatting with Jacob in the cafe. The temperature has
dropped. Fall is here and winter will come soon. We would feel the cold if
we were sitting outside for a long time. The cafe is a snug warm cocoon for
us. I know there are people nearby. I hear the clatter from the kitchen, but
the softly lit front room feels very private, an intimate space. Maybe that
is why our discussions have veered toward serious topics. Mercifully, Jacob
has not said anything more about my reading his letters before we marry.
I am incredibly grateful. And, maybe a little disappointed, too. Instead,
he seems focused on understanding my religious beliefs. I have told him
that my religion is woven into everything I think and do. He says he wants
to understand, so he will be able to fully know me. I want to understand
Jacob, too.*

*Today I spoke of God's will. I explained that I believe God has a plan
for us even if we don't understand it. We must trust in His divine wisdom.
I saw Jacob clench his hands and bite down hard on his lip. He said that
he can't agree. Jacob asked me what kind of God would allow his wife and
child and millions of others to be wantonly killed in the war. What kind of
God plans such things? Why didn't He intervene?*

I was quiet for a long time. I didn't know how to answer his questions. Instead, I asked him a question. Was he sure it was not part of God's plan for me to go to the library, look for a book, and end up toppling into his arms so I could meet him? Jacob smiled and then laughed. He told me I was acting like a Jewish scholar, answering a question with another question. This lightened his mood.

Today I told Jacob a bit of my family history, about my deep roots in Lancaster county. He was amazed that members of my family had immigrated to the area in 1717 and had remained for generations. I wanted him to know how enmeshed I am in my family, religion, and traditions.

We were drinking cocoa. Our mugs were on the small table we shared. When Jacob reached for his mug, his hand grazed mine. He said, "I'm sorry." And then he said, "No, I'm not sorry." He reached for my hand and firmly held it in his own.

I was confused. The words that erupted from me were, "I can't. My family. My religion."

Jacob trapped my hand in both of his. He told me he did understand that my religion supports and enriches my life, but his religion had made him a marked man, had deprived him of everyone and everything he loved and valued.

Jacob said, "I prayed and prayed during the war, but my prayers were never answered. I saw men mumble prayers right up to the end and then die. What good are prayers if God does not care? What good is God? But you, Anna. I believe in you. I love you."

I felt like I was looking through a kaleidoscope. Everything was shifting very rapidly into new patterns. It was all happening too fast. I wanted to comfort Jacob. I like Jacob. But do I love Jacob? Do I love Jacob enough to turn my back on what I hold most dear? We haven't known each other that long.

Why did he have to say those words and change things?

I quickly left the cafe. I had to leave. Did I say a proper good-bye? I don't remember. I'm miserable. I don't know what to do. Oh, I do know. I should run away from Jacob and stop this nonsense once and for all.

But . . . I desperately want to see Jacob again. I want him to hold me in his arms and hug me again. What a hopeless mess! Jacob is hurt and angry with God. He has turned his back on his religion. Is it too late for me to help him? If he were able to accept God again, would he be able to see what I see and feel as I do? Everything would make sense if he became a Mennonite. Is this a possibility?

CHAPTER 33

S ARAH SAID, "I skimmed letter 10. Jacob's response to this diary
entry is in that letter. I will read it now."

❦

LETTER 10

My Dearest Anna,

I fear I went too far too fast today. You were so agitated
and left the cafe so quickly. Oh, my darling, please return to
me. I promise to be more patient. It was too soon for me to
press you. But it has been so hard to be silent!

Anna, I do understand that you love your family and
religion. But when I held your hand in the cafe today, I had
to tell you how I feel. All your talk of God's will and God's
plan were too much for me. I reject the God who rejected me
and my people, the one who let evil take over the world. I
don't want to have anything to do with that heartless God. I
just want you, my darling. Only you.

Anna, I deserve some happiness. And sadness clings to you,
too. I know you live in the dark shadow of your sister's death.

Let me help you find some joy. I promise to dedicate my life to you, to treasure you and worship you.

You will have to accept me as I am. I will always have a Jewish identity. I will not let anyone take that from me. I fought too hard to keep it to give it up now, but I can't be a religious man.

Please, Anna, don't abandon me. Please give me the opportunity to convince you that we are meant to be together. Please come back.

Love,
Jacob

CHAPTER 34

Paula said, "Some things never change. Here we have a 1947 version of Romeo and Juliet. We are dealing with the age-old dilemma, can love conquer all when there are obstacles in the lovers' way."

Sarah added, "And like me, Anna hopes to make it all okay if she can change her guy, and Jacob writes that he can't change, not for anyone. I know this love story is not going to end in a happy marriage, but I find myself rooting for them anyway."

Ellen said, "I understand, Sarah, but I have to root for my mother who has to enter this story at some point."

"Still," Paula said, "we can understand Anna's and Jacob's pain. Why does love have to hurt? Why does it have to be so complicated?"

"If we knew how to make relationships easy and painless," Ellen said, "we could write a self-help book and make a fortune. My mother told me that I'd marry well if I was able to love with both my head and my heart. Anna may have loved my father with her heart, but she knew with her head that it wasn't enough. Anna was tied to her family and religion."

"And it was 1947," Sarah said. "People married within their own groups back then. It was much harder to defy the norm and intermarry."

"So, where do we go from here?" Paula asked. "Up to this point, we've been lucky. There has always been something to link Anna's and Jacob's writings."

Ellen said, "The letters aren't dated, but the diary entries are. Let's look at the ones that follow the October 24th entry we just read and try to find something that will steer us back to my father's letters. We do have a pattern. Anna writes the most about my father on Fridays after she sees him. Is there an October 31st entry? If so, anything of value there?"

Sarah said, "I worked on the October 31st entry, but there's not much to share. Anna had a bad cold, and she didn't go into the city. She was worried about Jacob. She was afraid he would think she was staying away because she was angry. The entry is short and doesn't say very much. She wrote that she, like many Mennonites, did not feel comfortable with Halloween and considered it a day related to witches and Satan. She plans on asking Jacob what he thinks of Halloween when she sees him next."

"So," Paula said, "Anna was planning on seeing Jacob again. That's significant. Anything else?"

Sarah said, "No. How about entry for the next Friday, the one for November 7th?"

"I looked at that one," Ellen said. "Not much to report. Anna's cold turned into bronchitis. She wanted to get word to my father to explain her absence, but she didn't know how without making her family suspicious. She was not ready to tell her parents about my dad. She only wrote a few lines. She must have been really sick."

"I think I've found something," Paula said. "On November 14th Anna wrote that Jacob showed up at her market stand, and I remember Jacob wrote about this in Letter 11. Ladies, I think we're back on track!"

"Good," said Sarah. "Read the entry and the letter aloud, Paula. I want to hear more."

"Okay," Paula said.

CHAPTER 35

Friday, November 14, 1947

Today I was finally allowed to return to work at the market stand. I am so tired of hearing Mother say, "Bronchitis is serious. You can't be too careful." I know she means well, but I feel better now. Thank goodness the doctor gave me permission to leave the house and work at the market. I was relieved but nervous, too. Nervous about seeing Jacob again.

This morning I did struggle with the boxes of eggs and baked goods I carried from our truck to the stand. I guess I do need time to regain my strength. I was busy pouring the squash into a bin when the early morning customers started to stream in. When I finished, I collapsed into my chair and looked around. I saw, much to my amazement, that the customer talking to Father at the other end of the counter was Jacob. I think my mouth fell open. How could this be happening? Jacob was always at work on Friday mornings. But there he was, purchasing one of our homemade shoofly pies. Jacob paid for the pie, turned in my direction, and spotted me. Surprise, delight, and then anger. All these rapidly flashed across his face as he walked towards me.

What I feared had happened. Jacob was angry because he thought I had abandoned him. I shakily rose from my seat when he stood in front of me. His eyes narrowed, and he said, "You've been sick."

I softly said, "Yes," conscious that Mother and Father, currently busy with other customers, were not too far away. I quietly asked Jacob if we could meet at the cafe in the afternoon.

He said, "I'll be there."

I was grateful that gossipy Rebecca, who was working in the adjacent stand, did not witness this quick exchange. Now, what does that say about me?

All morning and through the early afternoon, I alternately wanted to push time forward so I could talk to Jacob and wished I could pull it back to delay the meeting. When I was sick and had too much idle time, I thought of wonderful and witty things to say to Jacob. However, when my fever broke, those same things seemed very silly. I must accept my fate. I am a shy ordinary Mennonite spinster. I can't impress with my looks nor my words. I had no idea what I would say to Jacob to make things right.

As usual, the number of customers dwindled in the mid-afternoon. It was my break time. It was my library time. I returned my books at the library, checked out new ones, and looked for Jacob. He wasn't in his customary place at the table near the reference section. For a moment I panicked, then I remembered he agreed to meet me at the cafe. Jacob opened the front door when I arrived; he'd been waiting for me. I saw two plates on one of the little tables, each had a slice of shoofly pie on it. Beside each plate was a mug of coffee.

Jacob saw me look at the pie and said, "I heard it's a local favorite. I wanted to try it. It's very sweet."

I nodded, sat down, and stared at my slice. My mouth was so dry. I couldn't speak, let alone swallow a morsel of pie.

I sipped some coffee and then managed to say, "I'm sorry Jacob. I couldn't get word to you. I've been very sick."

"I believe you," Jacob said. "You look terrible."

Well, that did it. I was already strung so tight, worried about what I would say and do. I started to cry.

Jacob pushed his chair close to mine, wrapped his arms around me, and said, "No. No, little one. Forgive me. Those were the wrong words."

I sobbed for a while. Everyone wants to pretend I look alright, but I never will be as pretty as my sister Katie. That's the simple truth.

Jacob said, "I believe you were sick because you're very pale and have lost some weight. That's all. You're still beautiful."

I smiled. I couldn't help it. Jacob makes me feel good. That is why I had to pull my chair away from his and put some distance between us. I told Jacob we needed some guidelines if we were to continue seeing each other. I quickly came up with three rules.

Jacob was upset. He said, "But I met your father. He spoke to me. He liked me."

I said, "Yes. He liked you because you were a customer. He wouldn't like it if he thought you were more than a friend to me."

I told Jacob to think things over and give me his decision next week. I hope he will agree. What will I do if he doesn't agree?

CHAPTER 36

LETTER 11

My Dearest Anna,

Today I did something I have never done before. I left
work early. I told my supervisor that I was ill and that I had
to leave. I didn't plan on doing this, but I couldn't remain
at work one minute longer. I didn't lie. I felt sick. Yes, I was
heartsick with worry about you. I walked the six miles into
the city in record time. I can't tell you what I saw along the
way. All I could think about was you. I made up my mind I
would scour the market until I found you. I had to see you.
Too much time had passed without a word or sign. I had to
know you were alright.

It didn't take me long to find your market stand. Oh, dear
Anna, you looked so tired and thin. All my anger evaporated
when I saw you. And then, stupid me, I blundered with my
English. I said the wrong words to you in the cafe, and you
cried. I wanted to hold you in my arms and comfort you, but
instead I pushed you further away. Rules. Now you say there
are rules. How am I supposed to follow rules when I love you
so much?

* I cannot speak of love
* I cannot speak of a future
* I must give you time

This last rule is the most confusing! You say you need time to show me the glories of your religion and your life. How much time? And then what? Anna, I'm Jewish. I can't alter that. What do you expect to change or gain?

You are a timid bird who is afraid to fly far from the nest. I understand. But you are also a grown woman. You deserve a life of your own, and you can choose to share it with me. Right? Maybe time will work for me. Maybe I will have time to change your mind.

I think it's time I bought a car.

Love,

Jacob

"Now that's peculiar," Paula said. "Why does Jacob mention a car? How does that fit in?"

Ellen said, "I don't know, but my father often hummed a silly tune on road trips. 'Jacob's Jalopy' was its name, and I loved hearing it when I was little. Dad said the song mimicked the clangs and rattles of his very first car. He would add funny noises at the end to signal that the car in the tune had sputtered to a stop, and I would giggle. Gosh, that's a memory that goes way back."

"And your memory just jogged my memory," Sarah said. "I read about Jacob's Jalopy this morning. It's mentioned in Letter 12. And Jacob's discusses Anna's rules in that letter, too. Give me a minute to find it, and then I'll read the letter aloud."

CHAPTER 37

My Beloved Anna,

I am not breaking a rule. I will not say the word "love" to you, but you cannot fault me for referring to you as "my beloved Anna" in these letters. You were so shocked today. I knew I would surprise you, and I did!

I parked my car in front of the library. Only took me three tries to maneuver the car into the parking space. I tapped my fingers on the steering wheel while I waited for you. Finally, you walked out of the library, holding an armful of books, and I honked my horn. But you didn't react or look in my direction. I honked again. You kept walking.

There was no help for it. I had to jump out of the car and follow you. I was hoping you would see me behind the wheel, looking suave and confident, but the next best thing occurred. I caught up with you and steered you to the car. I opened the passenger's side door with a flourish and told you to please sit down, relax, and enjoy the ride. I could see you were amazed and confused.

"Yes," I said, "this is my car."

And you had so many questions. I told you how I bought my 1939 black two door Chevrolet for a great price and that the farmer who sold me the car threw in free driving lessons with the deal. You laughed when I said that I had given my "new-to-me" used car a name. From now on and forevermore, it will be known as Jacob's Jalopy. I like it. It gives my car an identity. The car does make some frightful noises, but the farmer said they are perfectly normal. He said those are the noises cars make initially when you are breaking them in. I hope he is right.

I think I was born to drive. Everything except parking has come easily to me. I love the freedom the car gives me.

I said, "Now we can explore!"

And you looked at me and quietly asked, "The rules?"

I could see the fear on your face, and I couldn't be mean.

"I will follow the rules for now. It will be easier with the car. We can have adventures and talk about them and not about us." This is what I said. Did I believe what I said? No. But I was determined to try for your sake.

Oh, what a ride we had after that. I circled the downtown and then headed into the country. We didn't have to go far before we were in farmland. You had so much to tell me. Your cheeks were flushed, and your eyes were bright as you described the families who owned the farms we flew past. You were relaxed and happy, and I was happy watching you.

I must admit I was surprised when you said you had a surprise for me, too. And what a wonderful surprise it is!

You had to return to your market stand all too soon. Anna, it did hurt when you asked me to drop you off a couple of blocks away from the market. You didn't explain. You didn't have to. You are afraid to be seen with me. I need to work slowly. I have changed so doesn't that prove that all things can change?

Love,

Jacob

CHAPTER 38

E LLEN SAID, "ANNA mentions both a surprise and my father buying a car in one of the diary entries I skimmed. The date on the entry is November 21st so it must fit in right here."

❧

Friday, November 21, 1947

What a day! I had my fears, but it turned out to be a glorious day. Jacob is willing to accept my rules. Now we can continue to be friends, but I must be careful. I must respect my church and my parents. I must!

And Jacob bought a car! I must admit that I was initially reluctant to slide into the passenger seat when Jacob opened the door for me. I knew Father would disapprove of me being alone in a car with a single man. But what could I do? I do trust Jacob, and I could see how pleased Jacob was with the vehicle and how much he wanted to show it off. I am weak. I reasoned that Father couldn't be hurt if he never learned of my indiscretion, and Jacob was right in front of me, expecting me to share in his joy. I didn't have the heart to hurt Jacob, so I quickly got in before I was spotted by anyone I knew. What a sorry old thing his car is. After hearing all the grunts and groans, I don't think that car has long to live, but Jacob is delighted with it. And imagine, he believes an eight-year-old car still has to be "broken in." He's so sweet and, despite all he has endured, so trusting.

It tickled me that I had a surprise for Jacob, too. A surprise as big if not bigger than his car! Who could have predicted things would work out so well? Before the market opened this morning, Rebecca's father pulled Father and Mother aside for a chat. At the same time, Rebecca rushed over to me. She was smiling and giggling and quivering with excitement.

Rebecca couldn't wait to tell me that she had met a fabulous fellow. This young man, the one she fancies, just bought a restaurant downtown and needs help on Saturdays. Rebecca's eyes were shining as she listed his many virtues. She spoke slowly when she described him, savoring every word. But then she gained momentum and rushed on, as if she feared I might interrupt at some point with an objection. It happens that Rebecca's father needs a new tractor. And Rebecca wants to work at the cafe. And what is needed is a friend to work alongside Rebecca. And . . . well, I could figure out the rest.

"Please, Anna," Rebecca said. "Do this for me. I absolutely must spend time with Samuel, and The Coffee Counter is a clean respectable place."

God works in mysterious ways. Jacob now works at The Coffee Counter on Saturdays, and Rebecca's Samuel is none other than Sam, Jacob's boss. Joining Rebecca means I will get to spend more time with Jacob.

Rebecca's father and mine worked out all the details. What an unexpected and wonderful surprise! And I loved the look on Jacob's face when I told him I would be working at the cafe.

I am tired. So much happened today. Thanksgiving is next week, and sales were brisk at the market. We will be even busier next Tuesday, the rush before the holiday. Will anyone invite Jacob to a Thanksgiving meal? I hope he will not be all alone. I wish I could ask him to join me and my family, but the feast at Grandmother's house is a ritual set in stone.

CHAPTER 39

"WHERE DO WE go next?" Sarah asked. "Is there a diary entry or letter that discusses Thanksgiving?"

"There seems to be a large gap between diary entries," Paula said. "I worked on the next one, and it's dated December 29, 1947."

Ellen said, "One of Anna's daughters kept the diary entries that dealt with family matters. She must have taken out the ones that covered their holiday gatherings. In the next letter, number 13, my father lists some New Year's resolutions. Paula, share what Anna was thinking about at the end of 1947, and then I'll read what my father had on his mind in January of 1948."

❦

Monday, December 29, 1947

The end of the year is approaching. I am content. Christmas is always a special time, a family time. I ate far too much, but I couldn't help it. All the holiday meals were so delicious! It was good to see the Ohio cousins. Rebecca had cousins from Columbus visiting her, too. One of them, Matthew, was very shy. He said little, but he seemed to absorb a lot. He is very tall. He resembles a young Abraham Lincoln.

Something totally unexpected happened today. I got a letter in the mail from Matthew. Father teased me and said, "You must have really impressed him." Naturally, I blushed. I don't remember saying anything significant to Matthew. He asked me to write him back and tell him about Lancaster, about the area and our farms. I will be polite and respond, but I don't understand why he isn't asking Rebecca's family for this information. That would make more sense.

Everything is working out well with Jacob. I see Jacob on Friday afternoons when I have my free time. Afterwards, he bakes breads and pastries in the cafe, and on Saturdays, we both serve the cafe's breakfast and lunch crowds and clean the kitchen. This is a comfortable and predictable pattern that I hope will continue. Poor Rebecca is terribly smitten with Sam, and, wonder of wonders, tongue tied around him. I have never seen her at a loss for words, but she just stammers and giggles whenever she tries to talk to Sam. Ordinarily, this would be funny, but my heart breaks for Rebecca as I can see how miserable she is.

I just looked out the window, and it's snowing. What a wonderful way to end the year, to cover the world with a pristine white coat. I hope it will last through the new year and not turn into slush. Right now, everything looks clean and fresh and ready for new possibilities.

CHAPTER 40

My Beloved Anna,

Everyone has been wishing me a Happy New Year. It is now 1948. I have heard about New Year's Resolutions, but I never have made any. You have improved my life, Anna. For the first time in a very long time, I am hopeful, so this year I will do something new and different and make some resolutions, too.

Sam teases me at the cafe. He claims I don't speak English "good." I wince every time he says this, and I want to shout, "You mean 'well' and not 'good.' You should use an adverb and not an adjective." But, of course, I remain silent. Sam says, "You don't sound like someone who was born here. You sound like you swallowed a grammar book." Ironic, isn't it, Anna? I worked so hard to learn the rules of the language so I could become an American, and now I sound like an immigrant because I know too much. In addition, American expressions are very confusing. When you said Rebecca was tongue tied around Sam, I worried about her twisted tongue and feared she would choke. Anna, I was so relieved when you explained what the expression really means. Why do words play such tricks, pretending to mean one thing when they really mean another?

My Resolution List:

Resolution #1 – Learn more American expressions

Resolution #2 – Reduce the number of tries it takes me to park the car in a tight space

Resolution #3 – Shave my beard

No need to explain Resolution #2, but Resolution #3, Anna, has been percolating in my brain for some time. It was always important for me to honor the biblical commandment in Leviticus and have a beard. When I was in Treblinka, the Germans shaved the men's faces and removed our beards to shame us. After the war, I vowed I would never let the Nazis conquer me again. But now I don't need hair on my face to tell me who I am. Anna, I am Jacob. I am an American. I am still a Jew. I am the man who loves you.

Which brings me to Resolution #4 – Convince Anna that she must marry me, that we are meant to be together.

Oh, Anna, I hope 1948 is our year. I hope you will marry me in the spring. The spring is the time for new beginnings. Anna, anything is possible. The letter I got in the mail today is proof of that. I can't wait to tell you all about it.

Love,

Jacob

CHAPTER 41

"Wow!" Sarah said. "What a coincidence. Anna gets a letter from Matthew, and Jacob gets something important in the mail, too. Both arrive around the same time. Now I'm assuming this Matthew is the same Matthew she wrote about in later diary entries, the one she married. I wonder if Jacob's letter is from a love interest, too."

"Oh my, that would complicate things," Ellen said. "I'm just wrapping my mind around the fact that my father was married to a woman named Esther and deeply loved this Anna, all before he met my mom. I'm not ready for yet another woman to be part of my father's love life."

Paula laughed. "Nothing you can do about it now, Ellen. It's all in the past and can't be altered. Besides, the relationships your dad had prior to meeting your mom may have actually helped their marriage."

"Explain," Sarah said.

"Well, you know the expression 'You have to kiss a lot of frogs before you meet Prince Charming'?" Paula asked.

"Yes," Sarah said, "I know that one all too well."

Paula said, "I think when it comes to love what's true for women is equally true for men. Maybe loving Esther and Anna prepared Jacob to really appreciate Ellen's mother. Maybe she was the final and best love of his life."

"I'd like to believe that," Ellen said. "But what if my father didn't follow that pattern. What if Esther was the love of his youth, Anna the real love of his life, and my mother was just a consolation prize?"

Paula smiled. "Even if we do learn that's true, your father, judging from all you've said, had a long, good, and productive life. And your mother was happy. Right?"

"Yes," Ellen said. "I think she was. But now I'm wondering if my mother knew about my father's previous loves?"

"We'll forge ahead and, maybe, we'll find that out. And I'd still like to learn what happened to that dented bullet," Sarah said.

"Remember," Ellen said, "a bullet is a small item. Maybe it was just lost. Small things are significant clues in mystery stories. They're usually not important in real life."

"Speaking of clues, my stomach's grumbling," Paula said. "I think that is a loud and clear clue that I'm ready for a dinner break."

"Sorry," Ellen said. "I lost track of the time. Tell me what you two would like on your pizza, and I'll call in an order. I have salad fixings in the refrigerator and ice cream in the freezer. Dinner will be served soon."

CHAPTER 42

ONE HOUR AFTER the pizza was delivered, all that remained of it was one small soggy piece. The three friends had moved to the family room to eat their dessert, and Ellen lit a fire in the fireplace. The trio devoured large scoops of ice cream covered with sprinkles and now were contentedly licking their spoons while the flames in the fireplace licked at the logs. The light from the fire softened their faces, adding a golden hue to each.

Sarah surreptitiously gazed at her cell phone. It was the third time she had looked in the last half hour. It was eight o'clock. There were no calls, messages, or texts from her boyfriend Rick. He had promised to get in touch by five o'clock. If they were going to go to the concert on Sunday night, Sarah needed to buy two tickets right away, but first Rick had to confirm that he could go. Why hadn't he called? Ordinarily, when this sort of thing happened, Sarah berated herself, sure something she had said or done had upset Rick. But not tonight. Tonight, she was angry. She hadn't done anything wrong. In fact, she always did more than her share, paying for herself and, more often than not, also for Rick. She was always bending over backwards to accommodate him and his moods. Why couldn't Rick show her some consideration? Maybe she should look for a better man. She checked the event's website again. She sighed. Now the concert was "sold out."

Not much got past Paula. She noticed the look of exasperation on Sarah's face every time Sarah checked her cell phone on the sly. Paula feared another loser boyfriend was disappointing her friend, and she understood Sarah's pain. Paula's ex-husband had disappointed her and her sons countless times. Just in case one of her boys needed her, Paula had also checked her cell phone for messages during dinner, too. She figured the boys' time with their dad would end one of two ways, and she couldn't decide which would be worse. The boys might return home and tell her they were royally spoiled and now preferred their dad to her, or they might inform her that their father ignored them all weekend and declare that they never wanted to visit him again. Paula couldn't envision a middle ground. She sighed. She feared she would have a lot to deal with on Sunday night.

Ellen noticed that her friends were distracted and waved off their offers to help her collect the dishes and load them in the dishwasher. She welcomed having a little time to herself to perform a familiar and automatic task as it gave her the opportunity to process everything she had learned about her father that day. It had been rough at times, but she hadn't fallen apart. Mark would be proud of her. She missed him. As usual, she was already listing the things she wanted to tell him when he got home. Ellen frequently had conversations with Mark in her head when he wasn't around. She knew him well and could anticipate his responses, but talking to Mark in person was the best. Not for the first time, Ellen realized how lucky were; they still enjoyed being together.

Ellen's thoughts circled back to her father. She had shared some good times with her dad, too. Jacob's Jalopy had reminded her of that. She pictured her father happily singing the "Jacob's Jalopy Song" on road trips to amuse her. The key was to get her father out of the house, where he hid behind books, and away from the pressures of the store, where he immersed himself in record keeping. Her father's habitual aloofness made Ellen feel unworthy of his attention, and she had cried as a child, lashed out as a teenager, and retreated as an adult. Still, there had been good times when he had softened. Why didn't she remember those times more often? Why did she cling to her anger more tightly than her love? Ellen sighed. She had been asking herself these same questions for years.

When Ellen returned to the family room a short time later, her friends were engaged in an animated discussion, ignited by her father's description of Jacob's Jalopy.

"Okay, Ellen," Sarah said. "It's your turn. Tell us about your first car. Did you give it a name?"

Ellen said, "I was in college when I got my first car. I inherited my mom's old Pontiac. It was a bulky gold four door sedan. I'm afraid I wasn't very original. I named it 'Goldi.' And I must admit, it was so boxy that I really didn't like it when it was my mother's car, but once it became mine, I loved it. Oh, the freedom it gave me! I think you always remember your first car."

"Just as you always remember your first love," Paula said.

"But usually the car is more dependable and lasts longer," Sarah quipped.

"Great gem of wisdom!" Paula said and smiled.

Ellen asked, "What would you two like to do? Work a little longer or stop for the night?"

"I'd like to learn what was in the letter Jacob mentioned in Letter 13," Sarah said. "We could solve that mystery and then finish up tomorrow."

Paula said, "I just remembered something. In Letter 14, Jacob wrote about hearing from a friend who lived on a kibbutz. His name was Chaim. In 1948 people wrote letters to each other. An overseas telephone call or long telegram would have been expensive. I bet the letter Jacob wants to share with Anna was written by Chaim."

Ellen said, "Let's find out if you're right. Paula, read aloud Letter 14."

CHAPTER 43

My Beloved Anna,

It's two o'clock in the morning, but I'm wide awake. I haven't been able to close my eyes. I wrote to you earlier, but I must write some more. I still can't get over it. I heard from Chaim today, and that is remarkable. I heard about Shlomo today, and that is miraculous. Of course, you don't know what I'm talking about, so I will explain. It's hard to calm down and think clearly, but I will try.

When I see you next, I will have to tell you more about my past. Not as much as I have written in these letters but a bit more so you will understand the miracle. Yes, it's a miracle. There was the Warsaw ghetto and Treblinka, and after that there was Shlomo. Clever, arrogant, and handsome Shlomo. But you don't know who Shlomo is yet.

You may remember that I once told you that a fellow *shohet* named Chaim brought me to Lancaster. We both got positions at the kosher chicken plant. Anna, I hope you remember this. Well, life for me improved because I met you, but Chaim wasn't happy here. His family was in New York, and it was a strain to travel home for *Shabbat* and then turn around on Sunday and come back to Lancaster. Chaim's wife has a brother who lives on a *kibbutz*, a collective farm, in Palestine, and he pressured Chaim. He said it was Chaim's obligation to help create a Jewish homeland, a new state. So, Chaim succumbed. Three weeks ago, he packed up his family and joined his brother-in-law on the *kibbutz*. I thought, "Shalom, Chaim. Enjoy your new life. I will never hear from you again."

Anna, today I heard from Chaim. You could have knocked me over with a feather! (I just learned this American expression.) I will copy some of his words so you can hear from Chaim, too.

. . . so, my friend, I was talking to this fellow who sat down next to me at lunch, and he asks me where I'm from. I tell him my story, and I mention I'm a shohet. *He says he once knew a* shohet *named Jacob who could cook but was a terrible shooter. He adds a little here and a little there, and I realize he's talking about you. Yes, you! What are the chances? His name is Shlomo, and he's a big man with such muscles you would not believe! He has a pretty pregnant wife and a small son. He's important on the* kibbutz. *People look up to him. He knows how to get things done. So, when I said I knew Jacob Friedman the* shohet, *he said I had to tell you that Shlomo is still alive and kicking. I promised to do this right away. I never would have guessed you were once a resistance fighter. Why didn't you tell me? . . .*

Now you know why I'm so excited, Anna. I met Shlomo after I escaped from Treblinka, and I joined his resistance group for a time. When I knew him, he was a bossy and brash teenager, and now he's a married man and alive and well and fighting to create the state of Israel. He's alive. I can't begin to tell you what this means to me. He's alive! So many died, but he managed to survive. Someone I cared for is still living!

I can't sit still. I keep jumping up and shouting and crying. I am bombarded by so many feelings at once. I said "miracle" before, and I will say it again. It's a miracle! I must tell you all about this. I must write back to Chaim. I must write Shlomo a letter, too. I'm so happy. I came close to saying "Thank God," but the words stuck in my throat.

Love.

Jacob

CHAPTER 44

"JACOB WAS SO happy to learn that Shlomo was still alive," Sarah said. "Isn't it wonderful? Shlomo learned that Jacob was alive, too."

"And," Ellen said, "we now know this is the news my father couldn't wait to tell Anna. So, Paula was right. The important letter was from Chaim."

"It's great to end our work tonight on a positive note. So much of Jacob's story has been so sad. I'm glad he got to experience something miraculous," Paula said.

"Yes," Ellen said, "this is a good place to pause. The guest bedrooms are ready for you. Just head upstairs and turn to the right. There is a guest bathroom in between them. Sleep well and we'll finish up tomorrow."

After her friends collected their gear and went upstairs, Ellen flicked off the lights in the family room. At the foot of the staircase, she paused to look at the framed family pictures that were hanging on the wall. A photo of her dad was in the center of the grouping. It had been taken at her dad's ninetieth birthday party. He was smiling, surrounded by family and friends. Ellen gently stroked the glass covering her father's face.

CHAPTER 45

"ANYONE NEED A coffee refill before we get started?" Ellen asked. Paula and Sarah simultaneously said, "No, thank you." Both still had coffee in their mugs.

The women had eaten an early breakfast and were once again gathered around the dining room table.

Sarah hadn't slept well, and she yawned repeatedly. She took big gulps of what remained of her second cup of coffee, hoping the caffeine would revive her. She had tossed and turned for a long time before falling into a restless sleep. Thinking about her boyfriend Rick had made Sarah feel anxious and sad. In the morning she had defiantly put on the "wow outfit" she had packed to wear to the concert, the concert she would not be attending. Today she was dressed from head to toe in flashy silver, and while she shone on the outside, she withered within.

Paula had slept well. Initially, she doubted that she would ever get to sleep. As usual, when Ron was with their sons, she worried about his behavior, but, Paula reminded herself, she and Ron were divorced. His new wife could mother and monitor him now, and worrying was not going to change anything. She mentally gave Ron a swift kick out of her brain, and that felt good. If Ron created a mess over the weekend, she had the strength and intelligence to clean it up. She was tied to Ron because of the boys, but he was not going to tie her up in knots any longer. Paula felt strong and content as she drifted into a deep slumber. In the morning she smoothed her wayward curls into a ponytail, put on some black leggings and a white tailored shirt, and was rested and ready to deal with Jacob and Anna's complicated romance.

Ellen was surprised that morning. Right before she fell asleep, she had been thinking about her dad, but it was her mother, not her father, who had commandeered the starring role in her dream. Her father had just been a member of the supporting cast. The details were fuzzy, but she remembered that her mother had hugged her and told her, as her mom so often did, to give her dad a break and to believe that he really loved her. Was her mother's ghost or spirit reaching out to her? That was a leap Ellen was reluctant to take. Still, the dream was comforting, and, Ellen hoped, a portend of good things to come. Ellen woke early and pulled on blue jeans and an oversized pink t-shirt, a gift from her grandchildren that had the words "This Grandma Rocks!" printed across it in neon letters. She was flipping pancakes when her friends trooped downstairs and joined her in the kitchen.

Now breakfast was over, and it was time to resume their work.

"Ready to begin again?" Ellen asked.

"Yes," Sarah said, "and I know where we should start. I worked on the diary entry that follows Letters 13 and 14. Anna mentions all the key items: the beard, Chaim, and Shlomo. Wait. I'll find it and read it aloud."

CHAPTER 46

Friday, January 9, 1948

Today was an "overflow" day! There is no other way to describe it. So much happened. Too much to fit into one day.

Of course, there was market. There were fewer customers today, probably because it was so cold. I wore my warmest clothes, but, despite this, my teeth were chattering when I entered the library. I quickly returned my books and checked out two new ones. I was anxious to see Jacob. We had agreed to meet at the cafe for coffee today before taking a ride in his car. I wish I could have invited Jacob to at least one of my family's holiday gatherings, but it was impossible. Tongues would have wagged. Everyone would have asked me all sorts of questions, and I don't have the answers yet. There's also something special about keeping Jacob all to myself. He is the first friend I've ever made on my own, and, for the first time, no one else is influencing me. Whatever I decide to do regarding Jacob will be totally up to me. It is both exciting and scary.

When I got to the dimly lit cafe, I was so disappointed. I didn't see Jacob. There was another fellow unfurling tablecloths with a snap and covering the tables with clean cloths. I was just about to ask him if he knew where I could find Jacob when I realized I was looking at Jacob.

Jacob without a beard. And such a handsome, younger looking Jacob! I must have been a sight, all red faced from the cold and wind and blushing an additional shade of red. Jacob rushed over to me and guided me to a chair. He rapidly told me that losing his beard was one of his New Year's resolutions. He also said something about a bird in the hand hiding in two bushes. He was so proud he had learned another American expression. I was too busy looking at his clean-shaven face to correct him. I must, however, remember to set him straight about it tomorrow. I have no idea how that expression relates to what he was saying!

Everything accelerated after that. Jacob put a cup of coffee in my hand, instructed me to "drink up," and then we were off for a ride in Jacob's Jalopy. I could tell that Jacob was anxious to tell me something important. He said he was looking for a quiet, picturesque place to stop, and once he found one, he pulled over. He grabbed blankets from the back seat and piled them on me to keep me warm.

"What is it?" I asked. I was getting worried. What could be so important that he couldn't talk to me about it in the cafe or while he was driving?

"Great news," Jacob said. And then it all came tumbling out. He told me about his friend Chaim moving to a kibbutz and about Shlomo, who was the leader of a resistance group in Poland during the war.

"It's a miracle," Jacob said. "Shlomo is alive!"

Jacob had tears in his eyes and a smile so wide it came close to breaking his face in two. I have never seen him so happy.

Joy is contagious. I was happy, too. Is this a sign that I'm truly in love. I've heard you're in love when another's happiness is more important to you than your own.

I floated on Jacob's good news all afternoon. Tonight, I'm wrestling with other matters.

When I returned home, there was a letter from Matthew in the mailbox. He writes to me every day. He is planning on coming to Lancaster next week and will be staying with Rebecca's family and helping her father fill an order for five customized desks. Rebecca's dad overreached. He always did small carpentry jobs over the winter to supplement the family's income.

Now he is in trouble because he accepted a large order with a deadline, and it's to be "Matthew to the rescue!" Funny, isn't it? Matthew didn't seem like much when I met him, but he writes the most beautiful letters. They do touch my heart. I wonder how I will feel when I see him again. I never expected Matthew to return so quickly. I was just getting used to him being a pen pal.

Too much in one day. So much to think about regarding Jacob and all he told me. Every time Jacob speaks of the war, he reveals a little more. So much pain and death. It is overwhelming! My heart aches for Jacob. And very soon Matthew will be in Lancaster, too. This truly was an "overflow" day!

CHAPTER 47

"I F ALL OF this were occurring in one of my romance novels," Paula said, "we would be approaching a turning point. The heroine would have to choose between the two suitors vying for her hand. Of course, there would be a fight or contest or something to determine the best man for her."

Ellen smiled. "I just flashed on a funny image, my dad in a suit of armor jousting with his rival to win the fair Lady Anna. Now, that would have been something to see! But back to reality. Where do we go from here? I skimmed Letter 15, and it deals with Valentine's Day. Are there any other January diary entries we should look at first?"

Paula said, "Actually, I worked on a partial entry that's not dated, but I think it fits in here. Anna wrote that she attended an event in January. It's really just a snippet. Perhaps Anna's daughter kept the rest."

"Let's hear it," Sarah said. "Share what there is, Paula."

❦

. . . and so, we again went down the road for a Wednesday night Singing. It has been so cold and dark this January. It's good to have something to look forward to at the end of the day. I do like singing and talking to friends. Matthew enjoys singing, too. He has a strong baritone voice. Sam and

Rebecca were nestled close together in the backseat. They've become a couple. Rebecca is once again a chatterbox, and Sam is proud and content. All is well there. Rebecca likes to tease me. Today she said we could have a double wedding if I'd just encourage Matthew a bit. Naturally, I blushed.

⁂

"That's all there is," Paula said. "Not much, but it tells us that Rebecca, at least, thought Matthew just needed a nudge to propose to Anna."

Sarah said, "I worked on the next diary entry, and it covers the end of February. Before we get to it, Ellen should share what Jacob had to say to about Valentine's Day."

"Okay," Ellen said. "I'll read Letter 15 now."

CHAPTER 48

Letter 15

My Beloved Anna,

Today is Valentine's Day. Yesterday, on Friday, I prepared. I baked heart shaped cakes and cookies.

I found some cookbooks in the library with pictures, and I experimented. I'd never made flowers out of icing. It was tricky, but Sam was pleased with the results. He put some of the cakes and cookies in the front window to draw in more customers, and it worked!

I am very confused. People say this is a holiday celebrating love, but it's called Saint Valentine's Day. Is it also religious? I didn't know what to give you today. There are these silly rules I agreed to, and I wasn't sure what you would consider appropriate. I wanted to ask Sam for his advice, but he, along with everyone else, thinks we are just friends. This is not true for me. What about you, Anna? You avoid talking about your feelings for me and claim you need more time. But when, Anna? When will you be ready?

Sam gave Rebecca a single red rose at work today. I would have liked to have given you a dozen or two or three! Instead,

165

I made you a small heart-shaped cake and put your name on it. I put it in a box and wrapped it in shiny red paper. It wasn't much, but it was something. You smiled and blushed when I handed you my gift. You said, "Thank you, but I have nothing for you." And I assured you that your smile was my gift, and I meant it. I would scale mountains for that smile. It's so frustrating to pour out my feelings in these letters and not be able to say a word of love to you. I hope giving you this small gift was okay. You have taught me that there is not one Mennonite way. I hope your church does not prohibit gifts on Valentine's Day.

I do enjoy our winter rides in my car. On full blast, there is just enough heat from the heater to keep us snug and warm. You don't think I notice what you've been doing lately, but I do. Somehow or other, you slide a religious lesson or two into each of our discussions. You look at me so intensely, begging me to accept your beliefs. I know your life and your choices would be much simpler if I became a Mennonite. I wish, for your sake, I could, but I can't. Please, accept me as I am. I promise you; no man will ever love you more or better.

Good night, my love. I will dream of you. I hope you will dream of me.

Love,

Jacob

CHAPTER 49

S ARAH SAID, "AND now onto Anna's diary entry for February 29th. Here's what she wrote."

⟨◈⟩

Sunday, February 29, 1948

It is the leap day of a leap year, and I feel I should make a leap, too. The problem is I don't know where to jump.

I must admit it has been flattering having Matthew around. He is very attentive and sweet. Now he is helping Rebecca's father sand and stain the roll top desks they built, but Matthew isn't happy. He doesn't want to go back to Columbus when the desks are finished. He says he doesn't have a place there. It's an old problem. He is the fourth son, and his family's farm cannot support everyone. The solution is simple to my father who does not have a son to take over his farm. The solution is simple to everyone in my family and my church. I can tell what they're thinking by the way they look and smile and bob their heads when I'm with Matthew. They're all signaling the same message, "Marry him." It would be so easy. It would please so many people. But what about me? What about my feelings for Jacob?

Oh, Jacob, I cannot stop thinking about you, worrying about you, and reliving the times you innocently held my hand and your arm accidentally brushed against mine. I dream of you holding me in your arms, not just in a hug of comfort but something more. No, I don't think of Matthew this way. Matthew is a lovely soothing lullaby. Jacob is a stirring symphony. The touch I yearn for is Jacob's. What am I to do?

ᴇᴏᴦᴀ

"Oh no," Paula said. "The next diary entry is dated April 9th. We've lost a whole month. What happened during that time?"

Ellen said, "If Anna's daughter kept all the March entries for her family, they probably dealt with Matthew and Anna's growing romance. We know she did, after all, marry Matthew and not my dad. I skimmed Letter 16, and my dad worried about losing Anna. He feared she was 'pulling away.' He mentions March holidays in the letter, so I think it fits in here."

CHAPTER 50

LETTER 16

My Beloved Anna,

I don't know what to think or do. I live for my time with you, our Friday afternoons and Saturdays at the cafe. You are the bright spot in my week, in my life! Why are you pulling away?

Ever since Rebecca untied her tongue and successfully flirted with Sam, she and Sam have sneaked out of the cafe early on Saturdays. This has given us time to be alone, to clean up the kitchen and sweep under the tables without being watched by anyone. We have been free to talk and laugh as we work. Then the best part. I get to drive you home. I always find an excuse to extend the drive. I usually park the car in a quiet place and offer you a special pastry I have made for us to share. I have been so happy, and you have laughed and blushed and looked happy, too. Why has this stopped? Now you fly out the door with Rebecca and Sam and leave me alone to clean up and drive home by myself. Why? What have I done?

Today I asked you for an explanation, but you were evasive. You told me you were needed at home and had to leave work quickly. Why are you needed at home? You told me not to worry. But I do worry. Our Friday time is still wonderful, but you come later and later and have less time to be with me each week. Why?

This has been such a strange month. I baked shamrock-shaped cookies for Saint Patrick's Day and bunny-shaped cookies for Easter. Sam told me that Easter bunnies lay multi-colored eggs, and adults hide these eggs so children can play a game. They hunt for them and then put them into baskets. This is very confusing. Why is there an Easter bunny? Why not stick with the more logical choice and have an Easter chicken? Yes, this is a small matter. I want time to talk to you about small and large matters. I want to discuss personal matters, too. I want to talk to you alone, not while others are watching us with judgmental eyes. Is it because of the Easter holiday? Do you feel the pull of your religion and family more at this time? Is that why you are changing?

Don't leave me, Anna. Give me a chance. I can't follow rules. I won't be patient any longer. I will talk of love. Without you, there is nothing of value in my life.

Love,
Jacob

CHAPTER 51

"Poor Jacob," Sarah said. "I understand his predicament. He was in one place with his feelings, and Anna was in another. When your love is not returned in equal measure, you feel so alone, so hopelessly lost."

Paula said, "But Anna was miserable, too. Her heart was at war with her head. And she was pushed and pulled by many people and obligations. Just listen to what she wrote on April 9th."

⁂

Friday, April 9, 1948

I knew it was wrong. I knew Jacob was impatiently waiting for me, but I made myself spend more time than necessary on shopping before I went to the cafe. I didn't buy anything I needed immediately. I forced myself to delay seeing Jacob because I wanted to rush over and fly into his arms. Does that make any sense?

Matthew is still here. The desks are finished, but he stayed on because of me. Rebecca couldn't wait to tell me this. Rebecca, Sam, Matthew, and I have become two congenial couples. I no longer am the "left behind" spinster who is pitied by the happily linked. I should be happy.

No, I am twisted and torn. I do not want to abandon Jacob. Of course, he has sensed that things have changed. He asked me why I no longer drive home with him on Saturdays. I couldn't tell him the truth. I couldn't say, "Because I'm afraid of my feelings for you. I'm afraid if I spend more time with you, I'll want to marry you."

Easter was the turning point. Matthew came to Easter dinner. Father beamed through the meal as Mother heaped second helpings on Matthew's plate. Everything about him is right: his religious views, his values, his work ethic, his love of family, and his love for me. Yes, he declared his love at Easter. It was a calm and steady progression to his proposal. I asked for a little more time. We haven't known each other all that long, and Matthew reluctantly agreed.

This is hard. After Katie's death, do I deserve Matthew and the life he offers? Would marrying Matthew be a penance or a reward?

What about Jacob? I don't want to hurt him. What should I do to be fair to Jacob? Fair to Matthew? Fair to me?

CHAPTER 52

"THAT'S ODD," PAULA said. "Why would Anna consider marrying Matthew a penance? Did she feel loving Jacob was so wrong that it was something she had to atone for? Do we have any follow-up diary entries to explain this?"

Ellen said, "I'm afraid there is another big gap in time. The next diary entry we have is from mid-May. We should look at it before we tackle the next letter. I only had time to skim the first paragraph of Letter 17 before we broke for lunch yesterday, but I remember it starts off with preparations for a June picnic."

"I worked on the May 14th diary entry," Sarah said, "but I didn't finish skimming it before we began the matching process. I'm glad we've worked our way to that entry. I've been wondering how it ended. I have it right here, and I'll read it aloud."

⟐

Friday, May 14, 1948

I want to preserve what happened today exactly as it happened. Right away, when I entered the cafe, I knew something momentous had occurred. Jacob was . . . I don't know what to call it. I think he was trying to dance, but he looked like a horse stomping. He was trying to kick his heels (without much success). He clasped my hands in his when I came in and said, "Dance! I've never danced with a woman. But I'm a different man now. I'm not living in a shtetl *in Europe. I'm an American. I want to celebrate. Dance with me!"*

I was shocked. I said, "I don't understand. I've told you Mennonites don't dance."

Jacob laughed and said, "Then twirl. It's not dancing. We have to celebrate together!"

I couldn't believe it. He picked me up by the waist, held me close against him, and twirled me around the room. Round and round we went till we both got dizzy and collapsed side-by-side on the floor. Jacob kept laughing and shouting, "Hooray! Hooray! They did it! They did it!"

I was panting for breath. "What's going on?" I asked. "Who did what?"

And that is when Jacob told me that earlier today Israel had become a nation, an independent state. He was so happy.

"Do you know what this means to me?" Jacob asked me this over and over, but I never got a chance to reply. He was so excited. His face was flushed, his eyes were bright, and his words tripped over each other in their hurry to get out.

"It means my people have a homeland. They have the right to live in the land God gave them. They have a sanctuary, a place where they can put down roots, walk freely, and rule themselves. It is wonderful! Wonderful! Finally, a place for Jews to live."

I do understand being tied to a land. I am tied to our farm and Lancaster County. But Jacob's ties are different. He is tied to a people and a biblical place. He is tied to a culture even if he rejects its religion. I do understand more than Jacob thinks I do. He is part and parcel of his world, woven tightly into its fabric since birth. For a long time, I was hopeful Jacob would become a Mennonite. I prayed he would. He's a good person, and I want him to be saved before he dies. I tried to change him and hoped he would see the beauty of my faith, but it's not to be. He can't live in my world, and I can't live in his.

I walked into the cafe prepared to tell Jacob about Matthew. I have decided to accept Matthew's proposal. But before I say "yes," I feel I owe

Jacob an explanation. I must make him understand. I don't want him to hear about Matthew from someone at the cafe. So far, I've been lucky, but how long can that last. Rebecca's tongue moves faster than the spokes on a windmill during a storm. Sooner or later, she will let something slip. It will be better if Jacob hears about Matthew from me.

Jacob was so happy today. He deserves to be happy after all the pain and loss he has experienced. We toasted Israel's independence with glasses of apple cider, and then I had to go back to work at the market. I didn't tell Jacob about Matthew. I couldn't on this special day. Tomorrow. I will tell him tomorrow.

CHAPTER 53

"OH NO," PAULA said. "That can't be all. What happened when Anna told Jacob about Matthew? She must have written about it. How could she not have written about something so important?"

"Let's go through the remaining diary entries we didn't have time to skim," Ellen suggested. "There may be one or two that are out of order. Let's check before we go on to my dad's next letter."

Three sets of hands quickly shuffled through the papers in the diary entry pile. A short time later, three women sighed in frustration.

"It's just not fair," Sarah said. "There's has to be a diary entry describing the break-up. Anna wrote in her diary all the time. Look at all the entries we have set aside because they dealt with ordinary things and did not mention Jacob." Sarah picked up a group of pages from their pile of discards. "Like this long entry that describes a barn raising. It's interesting but not vital. Wish we could trade it in for one we could use."

Sarah disgustedly dropped the entry face down on the table. Much to their surprise, the women saw that another set of papers was stuck to the back of the last page. Something sticky had created a seal, and two entries had become one. After carefully prying the papers apart, Sarah triumphantly raised her arm and pumped the air. She had found the diary entry for Saturday, May 15, 1948, and she immediately read it aloud.

CHAPTER 54

A bad night. Little sleep. All night long I tried to find the right words to say to Jacob. I strung phrases into sentences and practiced them, but I was too tired to remember much and kept starting over and over. Nothing sounded right. I think I drifted off at some point, but I got little rest.

I couldn't believe it. When I got to the cafe, Jacob wasn't there. At first, I was relieved. I didn't have to find ways to avoid him until I could talk to him alone. "Where is Jacob?" That was the question everyone kept asking because we were busy and shorthanded. The breakfast crowd left, and the luncheon diners streamed in. Still no Jacob. Jacob was always on time. Had something happened to him? I was worried. I also was angry. I needed to tell him about Matthew. I was ready to tell him. I couldn't keep putting this off. I wanted to get this burden off my chest. It was suffocating me! And Jacob wasn't helping me. He should have been where he was supposed to be.

We all chipped in to complete the end-of-the-day clean up. Still no Jacob. Sam and Rebecca drove me home, but after I waved good-bye to them, I didn't go into the house. I started walking. The weather was fine, and Jacob's cottage is just a few miles from the farm. I was bound and determined to find out what had happened. Jacob was a responsible man.

177

He must be ill or hurt. Those were the only reasons I could think of to explain his absence.

Shortly after I knocked, Jacob opened the door to his cottage and invited me in. The only word I can use to describe Jacob was "strange." He looked like he was wearing a mask. There was not a flicker of warmth or recognition. He moved like a robot and politely asked me if I would like to sit down. I was confused. I didn't know what to think of this mechanical man. I expected, at the very least, an apologetic Jacob who would explain why he had let Sam down and had not come to the cafe.

"What's wrong?" I asked.

No response.

"What's wrong with you?" I asked more forcibly.

No response.

Jacob turned away. I grabbed him by the arm and swung him back to face me. He turned his face away. I kept saying, "Talk to me, talk to me" over and over. Finally, Jacob looked at me and said these words—I remember them well as they tore at my heart—"Haven't you heard? They're killing Jews again. They're always killing Jews."

There was so much pain in Jacob's voice. He told me that he had received a letter from Israel yesterday, on May 14th. On the same day we had toasted Israel's independence, he had learned from Chaim's wife that Arabs had attacked their kibbutz on April 4th and that Shlomo, Sholomo's pregnant wife and son, and Chaim had all been killed. Shlomo had fought so hard for a Jewish state, and he hadn't lived long enough to see his dream come true. And Chaim, poor Chaim, had moved to Israel for a better life, and his life had abruptly ended there.

I gently guided Jacob to the couch. I held him in my arms as he sobbed. His cries were a combination of gulps and howls. I have never heard a man cry like that.

After he stopped shaking and his ragged breathing settled into a normal pattern, I gently released him. Jacob slumped against the cushions of the couch. His eyes were closed, and his mouth was pinched shut. Tears still coursed down his face. When he finally spoke, it was as if each word was being chipped away from a piece of granite.

"I'm so sorry," he said.

I told him it was okay. I said, "Don't hold in the pain. Let it out. You can trust me."

He nodded. I watched him struggle to regain control of himself. And then, much to my surprise, I was buried in an avalanche of words. Words fell out of his mouth, so many boulders, rocks, and pebbles. Poor Jacob! What a tremendous weight has been on his soul. He kept saying, "I'm so ashamed. I'm so ashamed."

I kept assuring him that he hadn't done anything wrong, that he hadn't abandoned his family. He hadn't killed them. The Germans did. His secret changed nothing. Nothing!

Jacob talked for a long time. He told me things he had been afraid to admit, even to himself. Now, I have an additional burden. Having encouraged this sensitive man to trust me, he did just that. He told me his biggest secret. He put his broken heart in my hands. How can I back away from him now? God help me! I don't think I can. I think I'm in love with Jacob and have been for some time. But there's Matthew and my family and my church. What am I to do?

CHAPTER 55

E LLEN WAS SHOCKED. "What's the secret? It must be something important, right? Let's not waste any time speculating. We've looked at all the May diary entries we have, so I'm all for going right to my dad's next letter. I hope it gives us some answers. I'll read it aloud."

❧❦❧

LETTER 17

My Beloved Anna,

   Thank you for not abandoning me after I told you my secret. I do feel better. I find I can breathe a bit easier now that I've said the words aloud. And thank you for seeing me again and sharing this special day with me. You have no idea how overjoyed I was when you told me that your parents would be visiting a neighbor after church services and that you would have this Sunday afternoon free. Free! What a wonderful word. We were free to be together for the whole afternoon.

   It was a glorious June day. I prepared a picnic feast of Pennsylvania Dutch favorites. I brought fried chicken, dumplings, red beet eggs, pickled corn, cucumbers, and apple pie. Your eyes got so big when I fanned everything out on the blanket.

You said, "My goodness, Jacob, you went to too much trouble."

I told you that it was no trouble at all. I found a Mennonite cookbook in the library and just followed the recipes for you. Of course, when you blushed, you looked so pink and pretty.

After our lunch, we took a walk. I was respectful. I only held your hand when we were on uneven ground, but, you may have noticed, I chose a rocky path that necessitated a fair amount of hand holding.

You were so quiet when we returned to my car after our walk. I was quiet, too. I do not know what you were thinking about, but I was thinking about you. You are so good to take pity on such a flawed man. I still can't believe that after I told you the horrible truth that you did not turn away from me in disgust. I truly am horrible because I initially enjoyed my time in the Warsaw ghetto. I was happier there than I'd been in a long time. I remember I kept asking myself, "What's wrong with me? Am I some kind of ghoul? Am I a monster?" But all I felt was relief. I didn't have to wield a knife and kill animals. I didn't have to be a ritual butcher and bring home an apron stained with blood and gore. I could sit in my brother-in-law's bookstore and read to my heart's content. Over time, there were fewer and fewer customers, and I had more and more time to read. People wanted food, not books. So, most of the time I was alone in the store, and I sat in a corner and read. I buried my head in books and tried to forget about the war.

I know now that I was naive and stupid. I didn't believe the horrific reports. I didn't think the Nazis would really kill innocent civilians. I can forgive myself for being fooled but not for the way I felt. For a long time, I was happy in the Warsaw ghetto! It is so shameful. And, when Esther spoke with longing about returning to our home and our old life, I always said I felt that way, too, secretly wishing we'd never have to leave and go back. I didn't want to go back to being a *shohet*. Of course, when conditions worsened, I would have given anything to get my family out of the ghetto. By that time, it was too late. And now I live with this horrible ache that never goes away. On top of everything else that happened, I lied to my wife. I was a phony. Esther deserved better! And I should have been wiser. I should have saved my family or died trying.

What amazes me is that you listened to all this and did not flinch. You pleaded with me to forgive myself. You assured me that I was not responsible for my family's deaths.

Forgiveness. I've thought a lot about forgiveness. After the war, I was so angry with God. I couldn't forgive Him for doing nothing and allowing so many innocent people to die. And I don't think I will ever be able to forgive the Nazis for what they did. So, what do I do? I can't turn to God to forgive me. I don't want to ask God for anything. He ignored all my prayers during the war. So, where do I go for forgiveness? And how can I possibly forgive myself?

You helped. You looked at me and said, "I forgive you, Jacob."

Thank you, Anna. That meant so much to me. If you, who are so sweet and good, can forgive me, then there may be hope for me. Thank you, Anna.

Love,

Jacob

CHAPTER 56

THE THREE WOMEN were quiet after Ellen finished reading the letter. They each were mulling over Jacob's secret and how it had affected both Jacob and Anna.

"What's next?" Sarah asked

"I think I need a break." Ellen said. "Let's make some sandwiches and eat lots of potato chips and top it all off with chocolate cake. I could use some comfort food. Okay?"

Her friends could not argue with that.

⁓❦⁓

After lunch, the women were back at the dining room table ready to resume their work.

Paula said, "I know Anna and Jacob never lived happily ever after together, but they did share an incredible journey, a special romance."

"It's all good if the journey is meaningful," Sarah said. "If the man is a good man like Jacob and not like my boyfriend, or I should say ex-boyfriend, Rick."

"Is he the one who didn't call you last night?" Paula asked.

"How did you know?" Sarah asked.

Paula said, "I noticed you checking your phone a lot. I could tell you were hurt. Had Rick promised to get in touch and then didn't?"

"Right," Sarah said. "He's a 'get them', 'love them', and then 'leave them' kind of guy. I just didn't realize I had dropped to the 'leave them' category. Funny, just when he convinced me to care for him, he no longer cares for me. Life really isn't fair, is it?"

Ellen said, "It will be when you fall for a good man who is ready, willing, and able to be a 'stick with you' guy. Don't give up."

"Now that sounds like advice we both can take to heart," Paula said. "I think I'm ready to get out there and look for a quality guy, too. What do you say, Sarah? Let's promise each other that we won't settle. We won't stop till we find great 'stick with you' men."

The two women reached across the table and shook hands. Ellen smiled and gave them a "thumbs up."

"Okay," Ellen said. "I'm a witness. You two have entered into a sacred pact. You will use good judgment and find wonderful men to date, and you both are going to report back to me with fun romantic tales in the near future. I'm in my sixties, but I'm not a stodgy old grandma. I will need to hear details."

Ellen laughed, and Paula and Sarah did, too.

"Okay," Ellen said, "back to work. We stopped with Letter 17 and a picnic in June. Are there any June diary entries we should look at?"

"I'll look," Paula said. "We've got to find out how and when Matthew gets back into this story."

Paula flipped through the entries in the diary pile, and then she pulled one out.

"I think this one comes next," Paula said. "I'll read it, and then you two can tell me if you agree."

CHAPTER 57

Tuesday, June 8, 1948

*I've been thinking a lot about Jacob. I understand being wracked with guilt
all too well. I pray I find a way to help him forgive himself. I never realized
how unhappy Jacob is with his work. He hid that so well. Now that I
think of it, he never did say very much about his job. He talked about his
co-workers, but he never spoke about what he did at work. It isn't right! He
has punished himself long enough. I will have to remind Jacob that he is in
America now. He lives in a land of many opportunities. It is not too late
for him; he can change careers. Jacob loves books, and he is familiar with so
many authors. He belongs in a bookstore or a library, not a slaughterhouse.
This is so obvious to me. Why isn't it obvious to Jacob, too?*

*And Matthew. What can I say about Matthew? He has been patiently
waiting for my answer to his proposal. My parents are confused. They say
they will respect my choice, but every day one of them asks me, "What are
you waiting for?" I can't explain. They wouldn't understand. Jacob still has
a strong hold on my feelings. How can I say "yes" to Matthew when I care so
much for Jacob?*

I keep telling myself that all I need is time. Time to resolve this. But what if I wait too long and Matthew finds someone else? What if I wait too long and Jacob pulls away, tired of my indecisiveness?

What if I end up all alone?

⌒◦⌒

"Good work, Paula," Sarah said. "You found the right place for that diary entry."

"I agree," said Ellen.

"And, judging by some key words I just spotted. I think Letter 18 comes next," Sarah said.

⌒◦⌒

LETTER 18

My Beloved Anna,

Today you asked me why I'm still a Jewish butcher if I hate being one so much. Well, it's complicated. I told you it is all I know, the only profession I've ever had. But there's more to it than that. I couldn't explain it well when you asked, so I will try to make it clear in this letter.

There was so much hunger in the ghetto and in Treblinka. I was always hungry. Everyone was so hungry. My father taught me how to be a *shohet*, and it's a good profession; I follow honorable rules. Jews can eat the animals I kill. The chickens I slaughter become kosher food. When I was in the ghetto and in Treblinka, I couldn't do anything to help my people get food, but I can now.

Oh, Anna, I do hate my job, but I must do it. I must! I know you mean well when you tell me that I can work in a library or bookstore, but it's impossible. It's too late for me to change. This is the only way I know to help people, feed people. Can you understand?

Today, Anna, at the cafe, I saw you with a very tall man. You spent a lot of time at his table. Should I be worried? His

186

eyes followed you everywhere. Dare I say it? I am jealous. Am I being foolish? I'm not brave enough to ask you about this man. Someday I hope we will read this letter together, and you will laugh with me about my concerns. Someday I hope you will read all my letters with me, curled up beside me as I hug you tight.

Love,

Jacob

CHAPTER 58

ELLEN SAID, "It feels so strange to learn so much about my dad after his death. There are so many questions I'd like to ask him now."

"There are questions I'd like to ask Anna and Jacob, too," Sarah said. "I'd start with that dented bullet Jacob always wore around his neck. What happened to that bullet?"

Ellen smiled and then said, "Well, there are two letters left. The answer might be in one of those. Or it could be in a diary entry, but there are only three left that have the name Jacob written in them."

Paula looked thoughtful. She picked up the last three diary entries, fanned the pages out on the table, and then said, "The diary entries are dated, so it's easy to put them in order. I just quickly looked over the last letters, and now I think I know where they go. Why don't we try this?"

Paula adjusted a few pages to make room for the letters, slid them into place, and then said, "Sarah, read aloud the last diary entries for us, and, when they come up, Ellen can read her father's letters. I think I found the right sequence. Let's see if I'm right."

Ellen said, "That sounds like a good plan."

CHAPTER 59

*On Monday Father finally saw the doctor. Mother has been telling him to
go for weeks. She knew something was wrong. I knew something was wrong.
But Father is so stubborn. Said he didn't want to waste good money on
doctor's fees when it's just old age that is slowing him down. Today Father
finally admitted that the doctor told him that he has a heart murmur.
He keeps saying it's not bad, just a minor thing. But I can tell by the way
Mother's eyes tear up that she's worried. Father frequently is out of breath,
and he's so tired that he can't wait to crawl into bed at the end of the day.
Farm work is hard. There's no way for him to slow down unless we hire
more help. I see the pleading in Mother's eyes. Of course, there is another
way, and we all know it. Things would be easier for Father if I marry
Matthew.*

*If I marry Matthew. Mother doesn't understand why there is an "if."
Father says, "I trust you, Anna, to make the right decision." Father knows
me very well. His few words are more potent than all of Mother's pleadings.
Matthew is back in Columbus. He's visiting his family. He writes every
day. He plans on returning to Lancaster to help Rebecca's father with the
harvest. He doesn't pressure me, but he reminds me that it is good to marry*

after the crops come in, when everyone has time to enjoy a wedding. Rebecca incessantly chatters about her fall wedding. Everywhere I turn I hear the word "wedding."

Soon there will be fireworks and celebrations. Sam has decided to close the cafe on Saturday the 3rd. He thinks people will be too busy all weekend with 4th of July picnics and parties to come downtown for a meal. "Doesn't pay to be open." That's what Sam said. So, I will have time on Saturday to do what I must do. I've put it off too long. I will do my best to make Jacob understand why I must marry Matthew.

I will write to Matthew right now. I've vacillated long enough. I will accept his proposal. He's a good man. I like him very much, and I will learn to love him. I will do my best to be a good wife to Matthew and a good mother to our children. I will serve my God and my church. There is no other path for me. And I will continue to pray that God will forgive my sin even though I will never forgive myself. Oh, Katie dear, forgive me!

CHAPTER 60

Saturday, July 3, 1948

I will always remember this day as one of the most difficult and painful days of my life. I did what had to be done. I will record here what I said and what Jacob said. I need to do this so there will be a truthful record. If I just trust my memory, I fear I will alter my words to make myself sound better. Someday in the future, I may want to read these diary pages. It will be difficult, but I don't want to forget Jacob. I want to remember everything about him, even the way we parted.

I marched over to Jacob's cottage early this morning and knocked on his door. Jacob was surprised to see me. I asked him if he would like to take a walk. He smiled. He said he was very happy that I had come by. He asked me if I would like to come in for a cup of coffee and a muffin. But I declined. I needed to be outdoors to say what I had to say. I needed God's natural beauty to remind me of His majesty and my duty.

Jacob carried a blanket. We walked for some time, saying little. We stopped at the pond at the edge of the farm. Jacob spread the blanket on the ground under some trees, and we sat down to rest.

Jacob said, "Take your time before you have your say. I know it must be important."

Jacob always is aware of my moods and feelings. Will Matthew ever know me as well? Jacob and I were sitting side-by-side but not touching. I was looking at the pond. It was easier to look at the pond than at him. I knew that what I was about to say would hurt Jacob, and I didn't want to see the hurt etched on his face.

I don't remember exactly how I started, but I know I rambled. I wanted Jacob to understand that when I joined the church, I had made a decision that can't be changed. I gave up my proud, selfish life to be saved. I can't live any other way now. I need to marry someone who has also been saved.

"Meaning you can't marry me," Jacob said.

"Please understand, Jacob," I said. "I never thought I would meet someone like you. Someone from a different world who would touch my heart. And you did. And you do. But it's not to be."

I told Jacob that love was not enough to sustain us. I need my church and family. I have to marry someone who is part of my community. I owe my parents too much. I can't let them down.

"Stop," Jacob said, "and listen to me. I get to say something to say about this. It's not just about you. It's about us. We need each other. You haven't let me talk of love, but you know how I feel."

Jacob gently swiveled my shoulders to move me closer to him and then held my face in his hands.

"Look at me, Anna. Really look at me. I love you. And I think you love me, too. Marry me, Anna. Please, marry me. It's 1948 and times have changed. We can marry. We can have a good life together. You can keep your religion. I don't want to take anything away from you. Your parents will eventually come around and accept us as a couple. We'll make it work. You and I belong together."

I did look into Jacob's eyes and saw that he was sincere. He really believed we could conquer all obstacles together. I must admit that I was tempted. Then I thought of Matthew, and I pulled away. I had to pull away.

"What's wrong, Anna? Don't you believe me? Don't you trust me?" Jacob asked.

I said, "God, church, husband, and then wife. That's the order I've been taught. The vows to God and church come ahead of the marriage vows."

Jacob was having none of this line of reasoning. He stood up and began to pace. His hands were clenched into fists.

"Please, Jacob, forgive me. I don't want to hurt you. I take full responsibility. I enjoyed our time together so much. I should have stopped seeing you earlier. It was unfair and selfish of me to let things go so far. I'm sorry."

"Anna, tell me you don't love me? Tell me that, and I'll walk away right now."

"I can't do that, Jacob, but I can't marry you."

I stood up, smoothed my skirt, and said, "I will never forget you, Jacob. I want you to know that your friendship has meant a great deal to me and always will. You're a wonderful man. I know you'll find a woman worthy of you. A woman who's prettier and smarter than I am. And you can improve your life. You owe it to yourself to stop slaughtering animals and to work with books. It would mean so much to me to know you're happy. Don't be controlled by guilt."

Jacob stopped pacing and turned to face me. The pain on his face changed to anger. "What? What right do you have to tell me to change when you won't change? You let the wishes of your family and your church control you and keep you from me. What do you know about my guilt and the way it eats away at my life? I'm talking about life and death guilt."

His words hurt. I turned away from him before Jacob could see the tears streaming down my face. All I could think of was Katie. Dear sweet Katie. And Thomas.

"Wait," Jacob said. "I have more to say to you before you walk out of my life."

I had to get away. I started to run, but Jacob caught up with me and spun me around. He saw my tears.

"Oh, no," Jacob said. "You're crying. Please, don't cry. I don't ever want to make you cry."

And then Jacob hugged me tightly to him, and that simple act of comfort broke down all my defenses. I sobbed against his chest.

193

"Anna, I'm sorry I was so angry. It's only because you're leaving me, and I love you so much."

And all I could manage to say was, "I do understand guilt. I really do. I killed my sister Katie."

"No," Jacob said. "No. You told me your sister died in a car accident. You said the road was slippery, and the car hit a tree. That is how she died. You didn't kill her."

Jacob guided me back to the blanket, and he held me in his arms. I cried and talked and cried. Of course, it all started with Thomas. Everything started and stopped with Thomas.

This is what I said. "Thomas and I were always together from the time we were babies. He was my best friend and confidant. I told Thomas everything, but I never told him that it really didn't bother me when he became more interested in my younger sister than he was in me. We were still good friends but were no longer discussing marriage. Our parents, however, had our future all arranged for us. They wanted a merger of our lives and our farms and set a wedding date for us. Thomas and Katie had other ideas. I shared a bedroom with my younger sister and pretended to be asleep on the rainy night she took a small suitcase from under her bed, tiptoed out of the house, and climbed into Thomas' car. I knew they were eloping because they thought the two sets of parents would object. Katie was only seventeen, and everyone always thought that Thomas would marry me. I never told anyone that I could have stopped Katie from getting into Thomas' car and dying. I could have made some noise and awakened my parents. I could have tried to talk her out of going. She would have listened if I had pleaded with her. She usually listened to me. Instead, I did nothing. I was silent and let her go. I committed a terrible sin, the sin of pride. I had outgrown Thomas and wanted more, a more intelligent man who would be more than a good friend. I wanted a romance. I thought I deserved someone better and was happy to let Katie have Thomas." I was gulping for air when I finished. I had never told anyone any of this.

Jacob said, "But, Anna, you have to forgive yourself. You didn't cause the accident."

"But I sinned by omission. I didn't do anything. I didn't stop her. At the very least, I should have tried."

"Anna, you must forgive yourself. You were not responsible. Thomas and Katie had the right to follow their hearts. It's tragic that they were in a fatal car wreck. But, please, hold onto this. They had the right to make their own choices. Don't you see, Anna? You have the right to follow your own heart, too."

"I can't be selfish. My parents no longer have Katie. I can't add to their hurt. I'm the only child left."

"So, this is why you feel you must be such an obedient daughter, to make up for Katie's death? Do you really think your parents want you to sacrifice your happiness just to make them happy? That's not what loving parents want."

"There's more, Jacob. My father's older now and weaker. He can get help if I marry a farmer. It would destroy us all if we lose the farm that so many generations of my family have worked so hard to keep for us."

"I could learn to be farmer, Anna. I'm strong."

"Thank you, Jacob. I know you'd try, but farming's not the life for you. I'm tied to the land as well as my family and my church. I need a man who can share all three with me. I want my children to be part of my church and my community. Can you understand this?"

"Yes. I don't like it, but I do understand. You always circle back to the biggest obstacle, the church. I'm Jewish, Anna. If I were to change religions after all I've been through, I wouldn't recognize myself. I wouldn't be me. So, what now? Will this be it? Will we ever see each other again?"

"I think it'll be too hard. It's better if we don't. I won't go to the library on Fridays, and I'll stop working at the cafe."

"Tell me. I must ask. There was a tall man who looked like Abraham Lincoln. He came into the cafe, and you waited on him. He never took his eyes off you. Is he important? Is he the farmer who can help your father?"

"Yes. I've just accepted his marriage proposal. It was a difficult decision, but I'm convinced it's the right decision. We're going to be married in the fall."

"Is he good enough for you?"

"Yes. He's a good man. He's not you, Jacob, but he's a good man."

"Well, then, that's good. You should marry a good man."

"Thank you, Jacob."

"Anna, if this really is good-bye, I want to give you something. I don't have much, but here. Take this." Jacob grabbed the long chain he always wore around his neck, the one with the dented bullet attached to it, and pulled it over his head and put it in my right palm.

"I know you Mennonites don't wear jewelry, so keep this somewhere and look at it occasionally. Please, don't forget me, Anna. Everyone in my family is dead. I'd like to be remembered by someone I love."

"Thank you, Jacob. You told me how much this means to you. I will put it in my keepsake box, but I don't need a reminder. You'll always be in my heart."

Jacob cleared his throat and then said, "Okay, then. We'll part. It's funny, right? If there is a God, He must be laughing. He has a very strange sense of humor. I thought He was through hurting Jacob Friedman. What more could He do to me? But He found a way to show me there's always another gut-wrenching pain. He put you in my path, so I could fall in love with you, and now He snatches you away. How do I live with this?"

I was overcome. I didn't know what to say.

"I dreamed about starting a wonderful new life with our first kiss. Now that dream is shattered. Please, Anna, I'd like to have something to cherish for the rest of my life. May I have just one kiss?"

I nodded my head. I had nothing else to give. Jacob slid his arms around me, drew me to him, and kissed me. It was a soft but persistent kiss, a long kiss filled with yearning, love, sadness, and passion. After some time, his lips slipped gently off mine. The kiss left me breathless and desiring more. I felt all stirred up and confused. Matthew had kissed me good night several times on the cheek, and Thomas had once kissed me chastely on the lips. This was a kiss of a different magnitude. We both stood, and I moved to the side so Jacob could pick up the blanket and fold it. After that, we walked quickly back to the cottage. Neither of us said an additional word.

When we got back to the cottage, Jacob's landlords, the Weavers, were picking cucumbers from some vines planted by the driveway. They waved at us. I could not escape them. I had to walk down the driveway to leave the property. There simply was no help for it. We played the Mennonite Name Game. After Jacob introduced me and said my full name, they asked if I knew this person and that with the surname Miller, and then they went on to ask about others related to a Miller. The Mennonite community is tight, and families are all related. I was anxious to take my leave, but I felt I had to be polite. I must have looked a sight, all blotchy faced from crying, and, to top it all off, I had been seen taking an unchaperoned walk with a man carrying a blanket!

Finally, I managed to put an end to the conversation and walk away. I looked around, but Jacob was gone. He had quietly left while I was talking to the Weavers. He had left without saying good-bye.

CHAPTER 61

My Beloved Anna,

I will still call you My Beloved Anna because that is what you will always be to me. Four days have passed since you broke my heart. I haven't been able to leave the cottage.

We were supposed to be together. We were supposed to marry. How will I go on now? The thought of returning to work sickens me. I don't think I can go back. I've seen enough blood and death. Enough!

I look at this pack of letters. You thought releasing my emotions in letters would help me. Maybe you were right. Maybe I should have shown them to you. Now, it's too late. Too late for everything.

I'm writing this last letter as a farewell to you and a farewell to this whole process.

Anna, I remember my mother used to say, "Don't be angry with the sun on a rainy day. The sun will come out again and make you happy." I'm miserable because you're never coming back. I will never be happy again.

I hope the tall man is good to you, Anna. If not, don't hesitate. Don't be proud. Come back to me. I will love you forever.

Love,
Jacob

CHAPTER 62

My Beloved Anna,

I have never forgotten you. I loved you very much, and I still do. Because you asked me to, I wrote you many letters. I still have them. I keep them because they tie me to you. Two and a half years have passed since I wrote Letter 19, my last letter.

I am writing to you today because there are some things I'd like to share. I'd like you to know that you gave me the courage to leave my job at the poultry plant. I got a job, a week after we parted, at a floundering bookstore downtown, and now I own the store. I'm very proud of my store. I've turned it around, and I'm doing well.

You always were encouraging me to try new recipes when we worked at the cafe. Remember? You enjoyed sampling all the new dishes. Now I cook three nights a week in the kitchen of a shelter downtown. It's satisfying volunteer work.

Anna, you set me free. I left the *shohet's* job I hated and found a better way to be of service. Now I use a frying pan instead of a butcher's knife to provide people with food. I was so mired in guilt. I wouldn't have moved forward if you hadn't pushed me.

I always hoped I'd run into you at the library or see you
at the market, but I never did. Perhaps that was for the best.
What was there to say that we hadn't already said? In the
beginning, I was truly angry and lost, but now I believe that
the benefits of having known you far outweigh the pains of
losing you. I'd like to talk to you now, but I don't know where
you are nor how to reach you.

Anna, I want you to know that when I looked at the world
through your eyes it became a kinder and gentler place. I
needed that help. My war experiences had made me hard.
When I was with you, I was able to relax and be a softer
person. I don't think I ever would have opened my heart to
love again if I hadn't met you.

Now I want to tell you about Nina. I never dreamed there
would be another woman for me, and then Nina walked into
my bookstore. Nina is a history teacher. She's lovely and has
a keen mind. She kept coming back to the store, looking for
more information about the history of the city of Lancaster.
She asked me a lot of questions about the books in the local
history section. We started talking about other things, too.
She repeatedly returned to the store, long after she had
completed her research. I was surprised and delighted when
I realized that I had fallen in love with Nina. And, wonder of
wonders, she loves me, too.

Anna, I enjoy having this gentle, thoughtful woman in my
life. I thought it was impossible for me to love again after you
left me, but now there is Nina.

I'm not seeking your permission or your blessing or
anything really. I've bought a simple sparkling engagement
ring, and I will propose to Nina tonight. As I have no idea
where to send this letter, I will just put it with the others
I have written. I wish there was a way to tell you that I'm
happy once again. I think you would be happy for me. Nina
is special. She will never replace you, just as you didn't replace

Esther. Each of the women I have loved has touched my heart at a different time and in a different way.

I'm thirty years old now. Nina offers me deep calm waters. It's a mature love, but there is passion, too. We hope to have a family, buy a home, and put down roots in the Jewish community. Nina is Jewish but will allow me to, as she puts it, fight with God on my own terms. She's a good woman. Nina's a sweet, compassionate woman who understands me.

I hope you are happy with the tall man you married. Do you still have the dented bullet I gave you? Do you look at it and think of me? If you do, remember me kindly.

Anna, I'm not foolish. I know you will never read this letter. But for reasons I don't fully understand, I needed to write it. I didn't say the words "good-bye" when you left. I couldn't. I was still hoping you would change your mind and return to me. When you left, I was too hurt to say, "thank you." Those were the words I should have said. I would still be a lonely, damaged man if I hadn't met you. Because of you and the changes you made in me, I am hopeful. With hope, all is possible. And now with Nina, there is love again.

Thank you, Anna, for helping me to become a better person and for improving my life.

Love,
Jacob

CHAPTER 63

Wednesday, September 26, 2012

I'm thinking clearly right now, and I'm going to take advantage of this good time. I seem to drift a lot. I wonder if surfers who ride big waves feel as I do. A huge force just pushes me through time and then slides me back to the present again. I keep thinking about apple butter. Mother used to spread it on fresh bread, and I thought it was the most glorious taste in the whole world.

That's a Lancaster County memory. I have so many precious Lancaster memories.

Jacob will always be a wonderful Lancaster memory. My life is ending now. I can feel it. I am eighty-five years old. Jacob, if you are living, you are older. Jacob, are you still alive?

So many people have stopped by my hospital room to see me. I'm lucky I know so many kind souls. I prefer this form of passing, to die slowly rather than in a flash. It gives those who love me time to say good-bye and gives me time to tell the folks I love just how much I love them.

Here's my plan. I'm going to ask one of my twin girls to give Jacob Friedman my diaries.

But wait, what if you, Jacob, are dying, too? What if you don't have time to read years of entries? I will tell my daughter to keep the ones that relate to the family. That will help. In case you are still overwhelmed, I will make it easier for you and summarize a bit here.

I did marry the tall farmer, Matthew, and he tried his best to help my father on the farm. Unfortunately, Matthew badly hurt his right leg when he was pinned beneath our tractor. The doctors managed to save the leg, but it was weak. Afterwards, Matthew had a limp and had trouble doing chores, and there were so many medical bills. That's why my father ended up selling the farm. It became a housing development. After the sale, Mother and Father moved to a small rancher closer to town. They said they were content, but I knew better. They would laugh and smile in front of the family when they reminisced about the farm and cry when they thought no one was watching.

Many people feel depressed after they're hurt in an accident, but with Matthew, it was just the opposite. He picked the family up and moved us to Columbus so he could help one of his brothers open a modern grocery store. Matthew was optimistic. He said his injury was God's way of putting him on a new and more successful path. We had the twin girls, and shortly after the move, we had two sons in rapid succession. All, thank God, were healthy and beautiful and smart.

Matthew knew fresh produce, and he learned where to buy the best from nearby farms. Matthew and his brother worked hard. Their one store became a local chain. Have you heard of The Brothers' Market in Columbus?

I was right about Matthew. He was easy to live with, dependable and kind. I remember the night I panicked when Matthew was late getting home. It was a terrible rainy night. Katie and Thomas died on such a night. When Matthew finally walked through the door, I threw my arms around this neck and cried in relief. That's when I realized just how much I loved him and needed him.

Why am I telling you all this? Because I want you to know that even with a good man and a wonderful family, I often wished I could spend

203

more time with you, Jacob. So many times over the years, I wanted to run away to enjoy an afternoon in the library discussing books with you. Matthew was not a reader. I missed talking to you.

Jacob, I regret not saying a proper "goodbye." I meant to, but you walked away before I had the chance. More importantly, I regret not saying "thank you." Knowing you expanded my world. You encouraged me to think. No one had ever done that before. No one has done that since. It was wonderful!

Matthew died five years ago. I did love him, and I do miss him. Matthew didn't know it, but he owes you a "thank you," too. I think I was a better wife and mother because of you. I wanted to have an exciting romance, and, even though ours was small and brief by modern standards, I did have one with you. I fulfilled my wish, and I was satisfied.

I've written a lot. I'm tired, but I cannot stop until I tell you that I treasured that dented bullet you gave me. I kept it in my keepsake box. One day, when my sons were little, they drew a treasure map. I was upset when I realized that the treasure they hid was my keepsake box. I eventually found the empty box in some bushes. The contents were scattered all over the ground. I searched and searched, but I couldn't find the chain nor the dented bullet. I did spot a glint of silver between the twigs of a bird's nest, but there were eggs inside it so I couldn't tear it apart to investigate. I'm sorry I lost the bullet, Jacob, but I didn't need it. I never forgot you. I never stopped loving you.

I wish I had visited your bookstore. I was so happy when I heard you had bought the store. I'd think about stopping by when I was in Lancaster visiting my family, but I'd lose my nerve because I always was with Matthew and the children.

I'm sorry, Jacob, I can't write any more. I have resisted calling for pain medication for quite a while. I had a great deal I wanted to tell you, and I wanted to write it all down while my mind was clear. Now the pain is coming back. I need to call for a nurse. Oh, the pain is bad. Jacob, please believe this; a part of my heart will always belong to you.

CHAPTER 64

PAULA SAID, "I can't believe it. Sarah actually got to learn what happened to the dented bullet."

Sarah smiled, "Yes, I did. Imagine that. And Ellen was right, too. She said that such a small thing might have been lost over time, and it was."

Ellen was quiet. She was relieved to learn that her father's love for Anna had helped and not her hurt mother. Anna had softened her dad's heart so that when Nina, her mother, came along, her dad was ready for his final romance.

"I can't get over the fact," Sarah said, "that Anna and Jacob were able to fall in love even though they came from different worlds and were of different faiths. And then they parted because they came from different worlds and were of different faiths. Although the break-up hurt, they both felt that their romance had helped them. They each wanted to say 'thank you' to the other. That's the good part I like."

"But the sad part is," Paula countered, "that neither one of them said those words to the other. We know this now because we read what they wrote, but they never got to hear nor read those words of gratitude."

Ellen said, "It's remarkable that such a short, innocent romance had such a lasting influence on both Anna and my dad. What they felt for each other had to have been very strong."

"I've thought a lot about what happens after a break-up," Sarah said. "I hate to lose all the thoughts and feelings I've shared with someone I've loved. These are things that really define me, and it takes time and courage to divulge them. Then, when my guy leaves, off they go with him. I wonder what he will do with those pieces of my life. Will he treasure them, hold them up to ridicule, or simply forget them? And, if I keep losing pieces of myself, will there be anything left of me?"

Paula said, "Sarah, you've got to put those thoughts into one of your stories. Better yet, write many stories. You could develop a collection of dating and relationship tales. Romance stories for Millennials. It would be great."

Sarah said, "You might have something there, Paula. I could start with a story based on my break-up with Rick. That will take place tomorrow. I'll tell you and Ellen all about it on Tuesday."

Paula said, "Yes, good for you! You deserve better than Rick. And I'll bring the next chapter of my romance novel to our meeting. Now, all we have to do is convince Ellen to put aside her private eye mysteries for a while and do something with Anna and Jacob's love story."

"Slow down," Ellen said. "I'm still absorbing what we learned this weekend. I want to talk to Mark and our children before I make any decisions. I'll probably donate copies of the letters that deal with the war to a Holocaust museum. I also need to figure out what is appropriate to share with Elizabeth, Anna's granddaughter. She wanted to know more about her grandmother Anna's past."

Paula said, "I'm all for creating a book out of the letters and diary entries we merged. It's an unusual love story. And everything is here. Point and counterpoint. He said then she said. You do agree, Sarah? Right?"

"Right," Sarah said. "And we can help, Ellen. Just as we did today."

"Thank you," Ellen said. "You two are the best. I never would've gotten through all these papers so efficiently on my own. Thank you so much for all your help."

"We should be the ones thanking you," Sarah said. "This was great fun."

Paula said, "Yes, it was. But now, I've got to get home. My sons will be returning soon, and they'll be hungry. They're always hungry. I need to get dinner started. I'm also anticipating some emotional fallout from their weekend with their dad. But I can handle it. I'm prepared."

"I need to leave, too," Sarah said. "I want to stop and visit with my grandmother before I go home. Anna's descriptions of farm life reminded me of my grandmother's stories. I have questions to ask her, and now that I'm not going to the concert, I have the time."

"One thing I do regret," Paula said, "is that there were so many gaps between diary entries. I keep wondering what was in the entries Anna's daughter kept."

Ellen said, "I'm afraid there are some things we'll never know. I guess that is true for every story, fiction and nonfiction. We can only deal with the facts we have, and the rest is all conjecture."

"But," Sarah said, "don't you wish we could go back in time and hand Anna all the letters Jacob wrote to her and then give Jacob all the diary pages Anna wanted him to read? And, afterwards, it would be fascinating to interview them and have them tell us their thoughts."

Paula said, "I think Anna would be happy to learn that Jacob found someone to love and would wish the best for him and Nina. Jacob, on the other hand, might be upset to learn that the farm Anna sacrificed their love to preserve had been sold and that Anna spent most of her life in Ohio. That might have broken his heart all over again. What do you think, Ellen?"

Ellen replied, "We'll never know."

CHAPTER 65

THE THREE WOMEN stood for a long time in the foyer. Sarah had her backpack over one shoulder, and Paula's overnight bag was in her hand. Ellen teased her friends. She told them they were having a "Jewish good-bye," one that took forever to complete. They were reluctant to part and hugged each other repeatedly at the front door.

"Remember," Paula said, "Tuesday is just around the corner. We'll see each other again soon."

Sarah said, "That's right. And I have a bright blue outfit I can wear. How do you think I'll look with blue hair?"

Ellen laughed. "Probably like a cute Smurf. But you'll pull it off. You always do. Now, good-bye, you two. Thanks again, and I'll see you both on Tuesday night at the library."

Ellen closed the front door and locked it. She could hear her friends laughing and chattering as they walked to their cars, and then they were gone. The house was quiet. Too quiet for Ellen. She turned on the television to keep her company and sat down to wait for Mark to return from his California trip. The silly sitcom with its phony laugh track did not hold her attention. Her mind kept returning to the letters and diary entries. Like Paula, Ellen also yearned to read the pages Anna's daughter had extracted and kept for Anna's family. Did they contain something significant about her father that she didn't know? She was too restless to watch television and turned off the set. She had a nagging feeling that Anna and her father's story hadn't truly ended, that something was missing.

Ellen walked into the dining room. It was time to pack up the stacks of papers and clear the table. She found a small box and started filling it with diary pages from the discard pile, the entries that didn't relate to her father. Mid-way through the process, she stopped. She remembered that Sarah had pried apart some important pages that had stuck to the back of a discarded entry. She emptied the box and started over. This time she carefully examined the pages and shook each group before repacking them. A small envelope fell on the table. On the front were the words, "For Mr. Jacob Friedman's Eyes Only."

Ellen quickly tore open the envelope, extracted the note card, and read the words that were crammed into both sides of the card.

CHAPTER 66

Dear Jacob,

I feel like I'm slipping away. I can't hold onto a pen. A hospital volunteer is writing down every word I say. She has promised to never repeat what I'm telling her.

I want to lift a heavy burden from my heart before I die. Here it is—I really did kill Thomas and my sister Katie. I told you the truth before, but not the whole story. You already know that I didn't try to stop my sister when she rode off with Thomas in the middle of the night. But, after she left, the sin of pride overtook me. My younger and prettier sister was going to marry my beau. She would be happy, and I would be pitied. I thought, "This isn't fair. Katie should wait for me to marry first, and then she can have Thomas." I dressed quickly, went to the barn, saddled my mare, and then rode across pastures and through a small stream as fast as I could. It was raining heavily, but I kept pushing my horse to go faster. Faster. My goal was to reach the crossroads point first and flag down their car. I would talk to them and stop them.

I was so close when there was a clap of thunder. My mare reared up and then bolted through the intersection just as Thomas reached the point where the roads met. His car swerved to miss my horse. That is why his car slid into a tree.

No one else knows I'm responsible for Katie's and Thomas' deaths. I couldn't add to my parents' grief. I couldn't tell them what I had done. I had to marry Matthew to make up for my sin and to help the family. Matthew loved me and was satisfied with me. Whenever I was sad, he gave me space and never pushed. If I had married you, Jacob, you would have pushed. You would not have rested till you knew why I was sad, and sooner or later, I would have confessed and told you all this. You probably would have forgiven me, but I couldn't have that. Couldn't risk it. I can never forgive myself!

So now you know, and there are no secrets between us. Forgive me, Jacob. I know it's selfish to share all this with you now, but I do feel better.

 Love,
 Anna

      ⋄⊙⋄

Ellen stood very still. She hadn't expected this. Her father was alive when Anna died, but he never got to read this note. Was that good or bad?

"Oh, Anna," Ellen said aloud in the empty room, "I'm sorry you carried around so much guilt and pain, but how can I be sorry about the way things turned out? If my father had married you, I wouldn't be here. And the children and grandchildren I love so much wouldn't be here either. Love is such a powerful force. It can alter the course of our lives. But for you and my father, it just wasn't enough."

CHAPTER 67

Ellen went into the kitchen and checked the clock on the wall. She really wanted to talk to Mark, but he wouldn't be home for hours. She walked over to the refrigerator, opened it, and stared at the well-stocked shelves. Ellen asked herself, "Now, what would my mother eat at a time like this?" The answer was easy. Go for Jewish soul food, chicken soup. Ellen heated up a bowl of matzo bowl soup, and for dessert, she had a piece of *rugelach*, the Polish pastry her father made for her when she was a child.

After her quick nostalgic dinner, Ellen decided she would sleep better if all the letters and diary entries were safely stowed away. She returned to the dining room and finished putting the entries they hadn't used into the small box that was on the table. What to do with the bigger stack of merged letters and entries? Ellen hunted for an appropriate box but couldn't find one. She wanted the right size container to ensure that the letters and entries would be safe and remain in the proper order. Then she remembered the box upstairs, the one that had held her father's stack of letters. There were just a few extra things in it from her dad's desk, so it wouldn't be difficult to empty it. Ellen quickly retrieved the box from the closet in the guest bedroom and took out two boxes of paperclips, masking tape, a ruler, and half a ream of paper. The box was now empty, but she noticed something white sticking half in and half out of the bottom folds. She gasped when she saw it was an envelope, and the name written on it, in her father's distinctive handwriting, was *Ellen Singer.*

Ellen's hand shook. She was afraid to open the envelope. What could be in it? How had she missed this when she emptied her father's desk? But she knew what had happened. After her father died, Ellen was choked up with grief but still had to clear out her father's apartment. The only way to get the job done was to behave like a robot, mechanically packing boxes and sealing them up. There simply wasn't time to carefully examine any of her father's papers. She planned on looking at them later. She vaguely remembered dropping an envelope in this box, along with the stack of letters and other items from the top drawer in her father's desk, and it must have slid down to the bottom of the box. Ellen sat down on the bed in the guest room, tightly clutching the envelope. She could wait for Mark to come home, but, no, there was no way she could just sit there patiently waiting for three hours or more. She slid her fingernail under the flap, broke the seal, and drew out the letter that was inside.

CHAPTER 68

My Most Beloved Ellen,

   I am writing you this note before I go the hospice center. I can hear voices in the living room. People are making arrangements. I know going into hospice care means the end is near. And that's okay. I'm ninety-eight years old and very tired. I'm ready. I've lived much longer than I expected. I think after your mother died, I kept living for you, Ellen, and the grandchildren and the great grandchildren. They're all wonderful. They've made me so happy and proud. They're my legacy. When I ask myself why I survived the Holocaust, the answer is to have this family.

   Ellen, don't be upset, but I was once in love with a woman named Anna before I met your mom. Your mother knew all about her, and your mother understood. Really, she did. My love for Anna never interfered with my love for your mother. I wrote letters to Anna when I was young. They are here. In this desk. In the top drawer. I was a different man when I wrote the letters. If I remember right, I had a lot to work out. I was angry after the war. Very angry.

I never wanted to talk about the war. Your mother understood. I was able to shed a bit of the pain but not all of it. And, Ellen, I have more to confess. I was married in Europe to a woman named Esther, and we had a daughter named Rachel. They were murdered in Treblinka. I wish I had been smarter and had found some way to save my family during the war. I wish I had been richer and had the money to get my family out of Europe. I wish so many things, but things were what they were. Everyone in my family died, and I lived. It was hard, but I lived. I told Anna the story in my letters. If you decide to read the letters, you will know the story, too.

It was so easy to love the grandchildren and the little ones, the great grandchildren. I loved reading books to them and playing with them. I still love talking to them now and following their adventures. Why was it so hard for me to love you? I am ashamed. I wanted to be closer to you. Instead, I left the loving to your mom. She was such a good and loving mother. I told myself that she did enough loving for both of us. But I was wrong, Ellen. That was not right. I wanted to love you, but when I saw your sweet little baby face, I saw my Rachel. Same green eyes. Same coloring. Same expressions. You looked just like her. It tore my heart apart. I felt so guilty when I looked at you because I would remember that I hadn't saved Rachel. I turned away from you because it hurt so much, and I couldn't stop.

Nina raised you well. I always was so proud of you, and I've always loved you very much. I just didn't show it. I was afraid to. I didn't think I could bear the pain if something happened to you and I lost you, too. Do you remember how I panicked every time you were sick?

So, my darling girl, I will die soon. I want you to know how much I've appreciated the way you have cared for me after your mother died. You and Mark have done everything for me and more. Thank you! Please tell Mark that I am proud of him, too. He's a good man.

I'm going to put this letter in the top desk drawer. You'll find it because I'll make you promise to pack up everything that is in my desk. You always do as you promise. I couldn't have asked for a better daughter!

All my love,
Dad

⋯❀⋯

"Oh, my," Ellen said after reading the letter. "Dad, I love you, too."

CHAPTER 69

SEVERAL HOURS LATER, when Mark returned home, he found Ellen asleep, curled up on the couch in the family room. He kissed the top of her head and was about to cover her with an afghan when she stirred.

"Mark, you're home. That's good."

"Sorry, honey, did I wake you?"

"No. I've just been waiting for you and dozing a bit. I have so much to tell you."

"Did the weekend go well?" Mark asked

"Yes. In fact, it went very well. I learned a great deal about my father. Mark, he wrote me a letter right before he died. I found it tonight. He wrote that he always loved me."

"Well, I knew that. I could sense it. He didn't have to put it into words."

"But he did, Mark. I always wanted to hear those words when I was growing up. I wanted to know for sure. And now I do."

Mark sat down on the couch beside Ellen and gave her a hug. "I have a lot to tell you about my family and the funeral in California, too. But it's late. We should go to sleep and talk in the morning."

"Yes. Sleep first, and then there's so much to say tomorrow. Mark, let's gather the family for a *Shabbat* dinner on Friday night. I have a lot

217

to tell everyone about my dad. Afterwards, I want to go to synagogue. I want to say *Kaddish* for my father."

AUTHOR'S NOTE

A LTHOUGH *Love, Faith, and the Dented Bullet* is a work of fiction, I want to assure the reader that the work was carefully researched. The information cited in the novel about the Warsaw Ghetto and Treblinka came from many books, articles, and survivors' interviews and testimonials that I compiled and then verified. The United States Holocaust Memorial Museum was an invaluable resource. I also visited many other Holocaust museums over many years in both the United States and Canada. For example, I was horrified when I read, in a Canadian museum, about a Jewish Holocaust survivor who tried to reclaim his home after the war. After experiencing so much pain and loss, this survivor just wanted to return home and live in peace; however, the family that had confiscated his property did not want to give it up and shot at him and told him never to return. I could not forget this story, and it found its way into my novel.

Why does the world need Holocaust novels so many years after World War II? Because there still are Holocaust deniers. Despite the fact that the Germans kept careful records of the atrocities they committed, there are people who claim that the Nazis did not purposefully kill millions of civilians. We do know the truth. The Nazis killed 6 million Jews. They also murdered an additional 6 million people from other groups:

Gypsies, Serbs, people with disabilities, Soviet prisoners, Jehovah's Witnesses, homosexuals, and political dissidents. There is a need for Holocaust stories because the staggering numbers of people killed may jolt the brain but may be too overwhelming to register appropriately and touch the heart. When a character you have come to care for in a Holocaust story dies, he means something to you. He is not just one of a large nebulous number. You pause and feel the pain of this one death and then begin to fully comprehend the magnitude of millions of deaths.

I wrote a gentle multicultural romance to balance my protagonist Jacob's tragic World War II story. I learned that there once was a kosher chicken plant in Lancaster County, Pennsylvania. It no longer exists. I created a similar fictional plant, within walking distance of the city, to give Jacob, a kosher butcher, a logical reason to move to Lancaster where he could meet and fall in love with a Mennonite farm girl named Anna. I am grateful to my Mennonite neighbors who shared their life stories with me. They also told me about their mothers' and grandmothers' post World War II lives. The information in the book related to the Mennonites and their religious beliefs is based on my interviews and the many books I read about this religious group. Lancaster County has become known for its Amish community, but there are actually more Mennonites living in the county than Amish. I wanted to pay homage to the local Mennonites' strong ties to their families, farms, and churches in this novel.

I would like to take this opportunity to thank those who helped me with this project. Thank you to Eileen Blaisdell and Peggy Brown who looked over early drafts and offered advice and suggestions. Thank you to my advance readers for all their feedback and support: Gail Blumenthal, Richard Blumenthal, Dorothy English, Julie Goldemberg, Paula Kinney, David Kleinman, Lydia Pease, Bonnie Prawer, Martin Rader, Joanie Stavig, Marybeth Toole, and Linda Ward. I am especially indebted to Susan Barnes and Adele Ruszak for their insightful and helpful critiques.

I would also like to thank my family for their love and encouragement. My husband Steve is the love of my life and my tech support. He inspired me to "go for it!" My children, David and Julie, and their spouses, Erin and Daniel, have been wonderful and supportive all along the way. I also want to thank my grandchildren: Max, Nina, Lucas, and Sophie. They bring me great joy and enable me to balance my solitary writing time with fun playtime.

A special thank you to the folks at Sunbury Press who accepted my book and took a chance on an unusual debut novel that does not neatly fit into one genre category. Thank you for giving me the opportunity to share my special tale.

And I am grateful to all of you who read this novel and spent time thinking about the discussion questions at the end. Thank you for your part in making my dream come true!

DISCUSSION QUESTIONS

1. Ellen's relationship with her father is strained. How does Jacob's past affect the way he responds to Ellen? What factors cause tension between fathers and daughters today? Do you think fathers have a more difficult time expressing their love for their children than mothers do? If so, why?

2. Ellen, Paula, and Sarah are writing buddies and friends. Paula and Sarah are younger than Ellen and move in different social circles. What are the factors that would promote and hinder friendships among people of different backgrounds and ages?

3. Paula and Sarah have troubled relationships with men. Were the problems realistic? Sarah wants to help the men she dates and change them. Anna hoped Jacob would be become a Mennonite. Is it possible or desirable to change someone you love?

4. After surviving the horrors of World War II, Jacob is angry with God. How do you react to this? Other Holocaust survivors have said that their faith in God helped them get through the war, and they became even more religious afterwards. Do you think you would follow this path or Jacob's? What part does religion play in Anna's life? In your life? Is it a force that aids or hinders?

5. Anna feels she cannot shirk her responsibilities to God, church, and family. Jacob feels love should conquer all. What is your reaction and where do you stand?

6. Anna and Jacob fall in love in 1947 in Lancaster, Pennsylvania, a very conservative place. Do people look at and handle interfaith dating

and marriage differently today? How would this story change if it were set in a different place and time?

7. Consider the challenges people face when they marry into a different group. How do the following affect a marriage: different religious faiths, different races, different cultures, different economic positions, different political/social views, etc. What if more than one factor is involved? How do these factors complicate a marriage and the couple's relationships with the extended families?

8. Paula says that Jacob and Anna's story is a 1947 Romeo and Juliet tale. Is she right? How are these two romances alike and different?

9. Jacob and Anna feel guilty about the deaths in their pasts. Is their guilt justified? How does this guilt affect them?

10. Ellen wonders how her father would have reacted if he had read Anna's final letter. She wonders if it is good or bad that he didn't get to read it. What do you think?

11. This is a very innocent love story. Does it work without sex? How would it have changed the story and your feelings about the novel if more acts of physical love had been added? Did the romantic acts in it seem realistic for the characters?

12. How did you feel about Matthew and Nina? Were they appropriate spouses for Anna and Jacob?

13. Jacob used his friend Joseph's visa to come to the United States. How do you feel about this deception? Was it understandable and justified?

14. The author researched accounts of life in the Warsaw ghetto and Treblinka as well as records of the Treblinka rebellion. Much has been written about concentration camps, but people know far less about the six death camps. What is your take-away? Did you learn something you did not know before?

15. Anna's ties to the land are explored in this story. How does protecting the family's farm influence the choices she makes? Many Americans today are not tied to a specific place and readily move for a new job or to enjoy a better climate. How have our views of home changed? Is this good or bad? What happens to the family when relatives do not all live in one place?

16. Jacob tells Anna that he is not religious, but he still has a religious identity. He is a Jew. Does this seem contradictory to you? Judaism is often considered both a religion and a culture. Is this true for other religions as well?

17. Anna visited her family in Lancaster after her move to Ohio, but she never went to Jacob's bookstore. Explain why you agree or disagree with her choice.

18. Much of this story is told through diary entries and letters. Are these reliable sources of information? Are people honest when they record events and emotions in diaries and letters? What type of person records daily events in a diary? Have blogs, tweets, Facebook accounts, and other social media replaced diary writing? What is gained and lost?

19. Nests were mentioned several times in the story. As a young child, Ellen thought of friendships as nests, Jacob tells Anna she is behaving like a bird afraid to leave the nest, and there is the possibility that the chain and dented bullet ended up in a nest. Are nests a symbol for homes? How do nests fit in with the themes of this story?

20. At the end of the novel, how have the characters grown and/or changed? What have Sarah, Paula, and Ellen learned from reading about Jacob and Anna's romance?

ABOUT THE AUTHOR

Carolyn Kleinman is a retired English and English as a Second Language teacher. She has BS and MA degrees from the University of Minnesota. Carolyn has always been a reader and a storyteller and enjoys writing books that explore how people respond to life changing events. *Love, Faith, and the Dented Bullet* is her first published novel, and she is currently writing a murder mystery. Carolyn lives with her husband Steven in Lancaster, Pennsylvania.